SANDCASTLES IN THE RAIN
SECOND EDITION

BOOK TWO OF THE FOUR PART SERIES
SOULLESS

———————

SUMMER SELINE COYLE

S S E Publishing & Acacia Leaf Press. Rothesay

SANDCASTLES IN THE RAIN SECOND EDITION
Copyright © 2018, 2021 by Summer Seline Coyle

All rights reserved. No part of this book may be reproduced, stored in a retrieval system, or transmitted in any form or by any means without written permission from the author.

S S E Publishing & Acacia Leaf Press. Rothesay

ISBN 9781999463915

This book is a work of fiction. Any similarities to real persons either living or otherwise, and real events are purely coincidental.

It is not the author's intent to depict a specific region. The particular setting of the novel is not a relevant factor in the narrative. The emphasis is on the universal aspect of the social issues in the book.

The courtroom scenes in the novel are plot devices and do not represent a factual account of the judicial system where the novel is set.

Typing, Formatting, Technical Support: Lyla Coyle

SANDCASTLES IN THE RAIN delves into the oppression and injustice Sydney experiences in the courtroom. The controversial sexual assault trial exposes the classism, misogyny, and victim-shaming prevalent during one of the most self-indulgent periods in history. A doomed love affair blossoms despite tragic consequences. When lives are shattered by a nefarious scheme, unexpected alliances are formed. This is the second book in the SOULLESS Series.

SEXUAL THEMES, VIOLENCE, STRONG LANGUAGE.

SANDCASTLES IN THE RAIN
SECOND EDITION

BOOK TWO OF THE FOUR PART SERIES
SOULLESS

This novel is dedicated to my beautiful daughter Lyla, who is a joy and an inspiration to me.

Chapter 1/ The Return

The soiled remnants of a late snowfall clung to shaded corners of ochre lawns. Under the lethargic April sky, innocent crocuses peeked tentatively in vibrant purples and yellows. Fearful buds were growing on branches. University students in rainbow-hued ponchos and bell-bottom jeans made their way along Waterloo Row.

Audrey had been issuing orders to the servants all day long. Marge had not left the kitchen since dawn, preparing her festive-occasion treats. The back door creaked as it opened and Peggy stood shivering in her trench coat.

"Hi, darlin'. Good day at work?" Marge glanced up from her mixing bowl.

"Usual sort of day. Mom, let me take over. You look ready to drop."

"I swear you'd think the Pope himself were coming to visit." Marge wiped the perspiration from her brow with a paper towel and shifted her weight to her left foot.

"Sit down, Mom. Your ankles are going to swell up again."

"I'm so nervous with all this excitement goin' on, I can't even sit down." she sat on one chair and placed her feet on another.

"What is the rest of the staff doing? Why isn't anyone helping you?" she hung up her coat on the coat tree, picked up a cotton apron with yellow chickens from a hook, washed her hands and took over mixing the dough.

"Miss Audrey's in a snit. She's got everyone runnin' around like chickens with their heads cut off. The girls are busy polishing the silver, cleaning the rooms from top to bottom, laundering the drapes and the slipcovers, beating the rugs."

"I want you to take it easy. I can handle the rest."

"Bless your heart, Peg. You're a saint. They've got banners all over the front hall, the livin' room, and the dinin' room. They've invited "Miss Hoity-Doity-Linda-Butter-Wouldn't-Melt-In-Her-Mouth". Everythin's been washed, ironed, dusted, vacuumed, polished, and decorated. Fresh flowers in every room. His suite is better than the Royal Suite at "The Queen's"."

"I don't think he's going to notice a few specks of dust. I'm worried about you, Mom. This is crazy. Every time he returns from one of his long world tours, they put on a big spread. If he weren't such a doll, the whole staff would walk out. Miss Audrey gets so persnickety, she's impossible to please."

"I still like her better than Miss Mildred or Miss Annette. She's more fair-minded, more reasonable, and not as petty."

"I agree with you there."

"I don't mind doin' anythin' for that boy. Couldn't ask for a nicer lad."

"He's a good guy. His taste in women leaves much to be desired, though. Shy men seem to get stuck with whoever throws themselves at them, and, it seems, the type of women who throw themselves at men are always the most vile, despicable creatures."

"Him and that Linda...There's a mismatched pair, if there ever was one...Just like all of his exes...I remember that Kate one. She was a tough ticket."

"Kiss-Me-Kate gave me the creeps. I don't know why he settles for all these cheap bimbos. They've all been psychopaths."

"That poor boy got no sense."

"Dottie's so excited to have him back. She's been terribly depressed since Minette died. I think she's got match-making on her mind again, though. It always backfires, but she doesn't give up. She wants to see him with someone nice."

"Who's she got on mind this time, honey?"

"Miss Lea."

"She ain't his type."

"I know."

"Miss Dottie's gonna feel neglected with Princess Linda dominatin' Mr. Jack's time."

"He'll make time for her. He always does."

"She's gonna be needin' extra special attention, what with her friend Minette an' all."

"Mom, would you believe that, when Dottie went back to school after Christmas break, everyone acted like Minette had never even existed? No one acknowledged what happened. Not even the teachers."

"Shame on them. It's a real disgrace, that is. Funny how the Wilson girl started comin' around again after that."

"Darnelle dropped her, too. With Hilary away, she wanted a temporary follower until one more to her liking – prettier, more popular, and more docile – came along."

"I never liked that Darnelle girl. Thought she was better than the rest of us. Put on too many airs."

"Cold and condescending. She gave me the creeps." Peggy slid the baking tray into the oven, "That's the last batch of rolls."

"Just leave everything, honey. One of the girls'll take care o' the washin' up."

"How many for dinner tonight, Mom?"

"Twelve. Nine family members and three guests."

"Three guests?"

"Mr. Warren's been keepin' company with a pretty brunette he met at The Metro – Felicia Somethin' or Another."

"I can't keep track of all his conquests." she rolled her eyes.

"She bears an uncanny resemblance to Miss Sydney."

"I don't like to see the Goldsteins left out because of that cad. He's the one who mistreated Sydney. I never understood what she ever saw in him in the first place."

"Somethin' that ain't there."

"You got that right."

"Mr. Tony is the one who's invited Miss Lea here tonight."

"Mr. Tony's a lost soul. He ain't never got over that pretty singer. It ain't none of Mr. Willy an' Miss Millie's business whom he chooses. Mindin' their own business ain't never been their strong suit. Always interferin' an' controllin' his life. Poor lad can't breathe. Sad to see 'im triflin' with Miss Lea's affections."

"I like Lea. I don't want to see her hurt, but it's inevitable." Peggy sealed the final tray of hors d'oeuvres with plastic wrap and placed it in the refrigerator. "Jack's going to be hurt, too. I just know it. I'll be watching this new gold-digger closely."

"She might be nothin' more than another flash in the pan. Some of Mr. Jack's marriages lasted no longer than one of my bouts of bursitis."

"I think I'll go downstairs, get showered and changed into my server's uniform. You, keep your feet up and rest."

* * *

To the amusement of spectators, Jack lifted Dottie up in the air and twirled her around.

"Jack! God, how I missed you!" she squealed in delight.

"I've missed you, too, little cousin!" he put her back down, and placing an arm around her, approached Audrey.

"Cut it out, you two. You're acting like children." Audrey admonished them.

"Hi, Mom!" Jack kissed her cheek and embraced her.

"It's good to have you back, darling." she kissed him.

"I'll be sticking around for a while this time." he placed an arm around each one of them and strolled toward the luggage carousel.

"I wish you could stay around on a permanent basis." Dottie said.

"I'm slowing down, sweetie. No more international tours. From now on, it's just going to be U.S. tours for several months at a time."

"Yay!" she spotted two of his suitcases and loaded them onto the luggage cart she had been wheeling.

"What's this I hear about you moving out, dear?" Audrey knitted her brow.

"I'm a big boy, now, Mom." he winked at Dottie.

"But you have a lovely private suite at home. Why would you want to live in an apartment?"

"Linda's found us a very nice apartment in a clean, modern building practically around the corner from the house."

"Avenue Towers!" Dottie hugged him, "That building's gorgeous! I've always wanted to see what it looked like inside. Aunt Audrey, it's the white stucco one with balconies on University Avenue."

"I know which one it is."

"At least he's not moving into one of those stuffy red brick wartime boxes with six foot ceilings and storm windows with three little holes."

"All the same, it doesn't make sense to me." Audrey shook her head, "And, living in sin."

"Mom, everyone's living together before marriage these days."

"That doesn't make it right."

"Why don't we get going?" he wheeled the cart toward the door, "I can't wait to see the rest of the gang."

"Everyone's dying to see you."

"I hope you didn't go to a lot of trouble for me." he navigated the cart through the automatic door.

Ryan was standing beside Audrey's white Mercedes Benz. He proceeded to load Jack's luggage into the trunk as Jack held the back door open for Audrey before taking the front passenger's seat. Dottie resumed her seat beside Audrey. Ryan returned the cart to the terminal and resumed the driver's seat.

"Thanks for keeping me up to date on what's been happening, Dottie." Jack said, "I'm still reeling from the whirlwind romance between Warren and my new singer."

"Tempest in a teacup." Audrey dismissed it with a wave of her hand, "They've broken up, and gone their separate ways. All of us could see it coming."

"Sydney must've come to her senses." Jack said.

"She was too good for him." Dottie said, "I love Warren to pieces – but, when it comes to women, he's got no scruples. Sydney's a very sensitive soul, and often misunderstood."

Audrey shot a disapproving glance at Dottie.

"Tony has a new companion." Audrey stated stiffly, "A school teacher named Lea Norbert. Mousy little thing. A plain French woman like Adele. Hopefully, he's forgotten about that Brett Morrow."

"Mom." Jack said sternly.

"Don't get me wrong, dear. I have nothing against Brett. She's got spunk. But she's hardly Horncastle material. Your generation's upset the dynamics of this family. You and all your strumpets: Tony and Brett; Warren and his countless conquests."

"Sydney was different." Dottie intervened.

"I do have to admit she was a decent sort. I suppose you'll be next, Dorothy: You'll bring home degenerates and addicts."

"Dottie's much too sensible for that." Jack said, "Tony, Warren, and I – we'll grow up eventually, and settle down. You'll see."

"I shan't hold my breath."

"So, my little cousin's graduating this year." Jack turned back to look at Dottie.

"I was afraid you'd miss it."

"Do you think I'd miss my Dottie's graduation? I would move heaven and earth to be back here on time!"

"Thanks, Jack."

"You'll do fine at E.C.U. next year."

"Thanks for the vote of confidence. Mom and Dad think I'll fail miserably."

"Nonsense."

"I've talked Sydney into taking some courses, too, so I'll have someone to hang out with."

"Sounds like a great idea."

They were driving past the Texaco gas station by Acacia Court, an upscale cul-de-sac. As they rounded the corner to Waterloo Row, the trees on their lawn, festooned with green and white balloons, were visible. The front door was open. Once Ryan drove up the circular driveway, the shrieking mob burst outside. A striking thin brunette pushed her way through the wall of family members and flung her arms around Jack the moment he stepped out of the car.

"Darling! Here at long last!" she kissed him.

"It's great to be back and see all of you." he attempted to break away from her.

Linda arched her fashionably thick eyebrows in pique and tossed back her waist-length hair. Warren eyed her in amusement.

Jack embraced Mildred and Annette, and struck up a conversation with Tony by the door. Linda approached Audrey and hugged her with an instant plastic smile.

"Audrey, how nice to see you!" she cooed.

"Nice to see you, too, Linda." she forced a crooked smile, wriggling free from her.

The younger woman sensed Warren's eyes following her as she strode into the house, her chin tilted upwards, her shoulders thrown back, her hair swinging behind her. In the living room, she approached Shawn at the bar and ordered a rum and coke. Warren came up behind her and ordered scotch. She glanced sideways at him. Drink in hand, she strolled, with cat-like movements of her lithe body, out of the room toward the solarium, and through the French doors to the patio. She placed her drink on the white iron lacework table. With graceful movements, she removed a pack of cigarettes and a lighter from her pocketbook slung over her shoulder, and lit up a cigarette. She took a long, languorous drag and gazed into the distance, at the barren silhouettes of the trees against a blinding coral sunset.

"Nice evening." Warren was leaning against a pillar.

"It was kind of stuffy in there." she responded, half turning her face to him.

"The clan's preoccupied with the prodigal son."

"I think I was expected to make nice with that frumpy old maid. I knew I had to get out of there. Who let that dog in, anyway?"

"I assume you're referring to Tony's date, Lea."

"Tony's obviously slumming it since he let that sexpot Brett get away."

"The femme fatale of Beavertown." he smirked.

"I hope I can look that good when I'm her age."

"Brett's appeal's highly overrated. And so is Jack's, for that matter."

"That's all going to change now. There'll be no room for his groupies. They can admire him from afar, but, at the end of the day, he's all mine."

"You keep him on a short leash, don't you?"

"I heard you broke up with your main squeeze."

"She was getting too clingy. I had to cut her loose."

"Clinging vines are like annoying insects. They need to be struck."

"She was suffocating me. I couldn't breathe."

"She's a loser. Who ever heard of a woman named Sydney? She wasn't woman enough for you."

"Is Jack man enough for you?"

"Wouldn't you like to know?" she butted out her cigarette on the metal table.

"What do you say you and I have a little stroll? There's plenty of time before dinner's served. I doubt they'll even miss us." he offered his arm, which she took without hesitation.

"Would you like to see our apartment?"

"Why not?" he led her across the courtyard and down the walkway to the sidewalk.

"I could show you my decorating skills."

"You possess other skills you could, no doubt, show me as well."

"Don't be crass." she shot up a glance at him.

"Who? Me? Mr. Charm School?"

Set back from both streets, "Avenue Towers" stood proud, fastidiously clean, and indestructible, surrounded by mature elms and maples on a large corner lot. Its pristine exterior and mid-century architecture with understated elegance was reminiscent of a more genteel bygone era.

"Come on up." she gave him a crooked smile.

"Promise to behave?"

"Do you?"

She unlocked the security door, led him into the white and green faux marble lobby, and up the white stairs to the third floor. The hallway had a green, black and white terrazzo floor in a flagstone pattern. The walls were painted a quince green. Two fire extinguishers were placed strategically at opposite ends of one wall, one of them beside the fire alarm box, the tool of many a mischief-maker. Pneumatic landscapes were hanging on the walls. Linda unlocked the white door marked 33, and switched on the lights to reveal a royal blue and scarlet contemporary décor.

"Very chic." he remarked.

"I adore the Post-Modernist Wave. I'm not into the earth tones, plaids and macramé."

"You have very good taste."

"Like a drink? The wet bar's fully stocked."

"Maybe another time. Show me the rest of the apartment."

"I may just want to keep you in suspense till the next time."

"You seem confident that there's going to be a return visit."

"Not just one."

"You don't lack any confidence, do you?"

"You talk too much." she kicked the door shut and seized him by the collar, pulling him to herself for a kiss.

Kicking off her red stilettos, she unbuttoned his shirt and bit his chest. He unzipped her tailored mini dress. She writhed around until she freed herself from it, and unzipped his trousers. With a leap of her svelte body, she wrapped her legs around him. He threw her on the bear skin rug and effortlessly glided into her. She devoured him with savage bites. Her legs wound around his neck, she pulled at his mane with every thrust. Still moaning in the afterglow, her hair was spread out like a sun spoke on the rug, beads of perspiration shimmering on her breasts. He sprang to his feet and began dressing.

"Linda, we need to get back for dinner, or they'll send out a search party."

"Let them!" she laughed demonically, "You think I'm dreadful, don't you?" she smiled deliciously, twirling a strand of her long hair between her fingers.

"Why? Just because you fuck your fiancé's uncle on the night the unsuspecting schnook returns home?"

She roared in laughter as she rose to her feet and danced in the nude.

"Get dressed, Linda." he said coldly, "Or I'll leave without you."

"Go ahead. It wouldn't look good if we arrived together, anyway."

"Is Jack really the guy you want to marry?" he smoothed his hair before the hallway mirror, "Are you sure you want to be saddled with the responsibilities and commitments of marriage?"

"I WILL marry him!" she snapped, eyes blazing.

"Of course you will." he winked and let himself out, letting the door close softly.

On his solitary walk, he observed the gold and red reflections from the North side of town shimmering on the river, and the willows quivering, huddled on the shore. His were the only footsteps on the lonely stretch of pavement. He slipped back into the house through the solarium as the family was being seated around the dining room table. Flashing his dimples, he took his assigned seat.

"Where's Linda? Has anyone seen her?" Jack inquired.

Warren shrugged his shoulders nonchalantly.

"Most likely freshening up her make-up." Annette remarked.

"We simply cannot wait any longer. The entrée is almost served." Audrey said icily.

"Please, Mom." Jack pleaded, "What if she's ill?"

"Would you like me to check the powder room?" Lea offered.

"You don't have to do that. We can get someone from the staff to check." Donald said, "Peggy, would you come in here, please?" he called out as he caught a glimpse of red curls in the hallway.

"Yes sir." the freckled moppet entered promptly.

"Would you please check to see if Miss Linda is in the powder room? If not, would you please check in the garden?"

"Yes sir." Peggy turned to leave, however, was stopped in her tracks by a flushed, flustered Linda bursting into the room.

"You can return to your regular duties, Peggy." Donald said.

"I'm sorry." murmuring with lowered eyes, Linda took her seat beside Jack, all too aware of disapproving glances from Audrey, Mildred, and Annette.

"Are you all right?" Lea asked in solicitude.

"I'm better now."

"Now we can get on with dinner." Audrey glared.

"I was worried about you, sweetheart." Jack placed his hand over Linda's.

"Just a migraine." she smiled reassuringly, aware of Audrey's unrelenting gaze.

* * *

Dottie hung up the cream satin gown in her closet and wistfully eyed the sky blue organza one Jack had bought for her in Los Angeles for the prom. Except, for her, there would be no prom. Those unable to secure dates were banished from the kingdom. Jack had volunteered to escort her, however, dates were required to be from the reptilian student body. The dress would undoubtedly hang in her closet for years, even decades to come, without ever being worn. The dreaded ceremony had gone remarkably well, despite the fact that it had been in the dismal hockey rink, the only building in town with the capacity to accommodate the families of fifteen hundred graduates. She had not tripped on the microphone cords or fallen off the stage. She had accepted her diploma on cue and shaken hands with the principal and the superintendent. Now, her release from prison was official!

Being coerced to attend the ceremony had been a bone of contention in the family. She still wished she could have skipped the entire evening and curled up in bed with a book. Her family would have none of it. There had been no caps and gowns, and no "Pomp and Circumstance". The girls had been told to wear long dresses of their own choosing, and the boys, suits. Military music had been played in the background by a sullen brass band of aging men.

The gifts lavished on her by her family were generous, and greatly appreciated. She would never have the opportunity to wear so many necklaces and earrings, so many silk scarves, or to read so many books. Jacob's pink roses in the crystal vase had been delivered in the morning, and were now on her dresser. Sydney and Brett had given her records of Helen Reddy and Gloria Gaynor. They were the best gifts by far.

Clara was going to the prom with Edgar. Both were professors' kids, thus bound by an unspoken contract of solidarity. Darnelle had hornswoggled some nerdy boy from her super-brain chemistry class into accompanying her. She prayed Darnelle would not attend E.C.U., however, despite her brilliant mind, even Darnelle could not secure a scholarship generous enough to cover living expenses as well as tuition at any other university. She would be forced to endure her for another four years.

It had been a long-standing tradition for all Horncastle women to receive their degrees in Liberal Arts. She did not want to be the first one to let her family down. Even Aunt Frances, the notorious black sheep of the family, had somehow managed to obtain a degree from an obscure university somewhere during her vagabond years, squeezing time for classes between ingesting illegal drugs and partaking of orgies. Aunt Audrey had obtained a Master's Degree in Library Science from Mount Allison, and moved to California, where she had met and married Ted Chandler, Jack's widowed father. Ella, a fourth generation Horncastle woman like herself, had become a Registered Nurse. Now, as the youngest member of the clan, it was her turn to prove herself. Or fail miserably, trying.

*   *   *

Brett locked the dressing room door and started toward the back door. In the unlit corridor, footsteps were heard coming from the corridor leading to the office. Her heart missed a beat. She quickened her steps in trepidation. The steps came closer.

"Jack? Is that you, hon?" she called out.

An icy hand came up behind her and rested on her shoulder. She let out a scream.

"Hello, Brett."

She whirled around and froze in terror.

"What are you doing here?"

"I came to see my favorite lounge singer, my best buddy."

"If you're looking for Sydney, she left after her set. She had a headache."

"That seems to be going around lately. No, I'm here to see you, Brett, old buddy. Where are your manners? Aren't you going to invite me into your dressing room?"

"I'm too tired to trade barbs with you tonight."

"I'll bet you're never too tired for action. You've been holding out on me, Brett."

"I don't want to argue with you, Warren. I'm tired."

"All the fellows have been telling me what a fox you are. Now I want to find out firsthand."

"Why are you here, Warren?"

"For what I've been missing. My share of the action."

"Warren, I'm all tuckered out. I just want to go home and sleep in my own bed."

"That must be quite a switch for you."

"I'm not in the mood to argue. I just want to go home."

"Not so fast. I want what's rightfully mine."

She made an attempt to run toward the door, however, found herself in a headlock.

"You're not getting away from me that easily."

"Let me go, or I'll scream!"

"Scream all you want. No one can hear you. There's nobody here but us, Brett."

"Jack's coming back."

"Nice try. Jack's all tucked in with his hot tamale for the night."

"Warren, just let me go, and we'll forget this ever happened."

"Ah, but, I will never forget what you did to come between me and Sydney."

"I had nothing to do with that."

"Methinks you had plenty to do with it."

"You can think whatever you like, but Sydney makes her own decisions."

"With some manipulating from you, no doubt."

"You give me too much credit."

"You've been trying to cause trouble from day one! You've been working on her in subtle ways, discrediting me in her eyes."

"You've managed to do that all by yourself, Warren. You certainly didn't need any help."

"You're pretty smug, aren't you, Brett? You've got what you wanted all along."

"All I've ever wanted was her happiness."

"Don't be in such a hurry to celebrate, Brett. You can't make these trumped up charges stick, and you know it. That's why Sydney didn't pursue it any further."

"The only reason for that is the fact that Sydney's a caring, compassionate person. She gave you a break. It's far more than you deserve."

"No, it's because she saw reason. It's not rape when two people are lovers. She's going to come back to me. She can't stay away very long. Sydney's mine. All mine. She'll always be mine." he bared his teeth, "Do you hear me? You had no right to poke your nose into our business!"

"Then, you should have treated her better."

"She'll be back. She never had it so good."

"Don't count on it. Not after the way you abused her."

"She loved every minute of it. She's in love with me. She'll miss me. Where else is she going to get such great sex?"

"This is between the two of you to work out."

"Not as long as you keep meddling! It's payback time, Brett! You're going to face the music. Didn't I warn you not to underestimate the wrath of a Scorpio?"

"Can't we discuss this rationally?"

"You're going to get exactly what you deserve, bitch!" he pinned her against the wall, "You're going to unlock that door. We're going to step into your dressing room and have a little chat."

With trembling hands, she obeyed him. He shut the door behind them and pulled her to himself. He kissed her until she was gasping for air. His frenzied fingers tore the fragile fabric of her dress, and squeezed her small, firm breasts until she cried out in agony.

"You're going to love it!" he laughed demonically, "You've been fantasizing about this for years, haven't you?"

"Look, I'll help you get back together with Sydney. I'll talk to her. Please let me go, Warren. I promise I'll make her see she belongs with you."

"Like hell, you will! You lying bitch!" he ripped the strand of pearls from her neck; they fell like hailstones on the tile floor.

"No! Not my pearls! Sydney gave them to me!" she fell to her knees, gathering the tiny globes in the dim light as they rolled away from her.

"Shut up! Stop crying!" he pulled her up by her hair and slapped her cheek with such force, she lost her footing and landed face down before him.

"Get up, bitch!" he poked at her with his foot, "Get up!"

Her face stinging, she attempted to raise herself, but he kicked her in the ribs.

"Didn't I tell you to get up?" he pulled her up with brute force and pushed her against the wall. His hands closed around her throat.

As he released his hold on her throat, she coughed frantically, gasping for air. His fist made contact with her eye and her weightless body collapsed. He placed one foot on her back as she wiggled in a desperate attempt to get away. His foot flipped her over and pressed against her throat. He laughed maniacally as he unzipped his trousers. She was no longer putting up a struggle. She was barely breathing. He slid into her effortlessly. She remained limp and lifeless. When he dismounted her, he began to dress slowly, casting a final glance at her. He slipped away into the night like a ghost.

*   *   *

The bitter wail of the telephone awakened Sydney. She groped in the dark for the receiver on her nightstand, and spoke groggily in a soft tone to avoid awakening her parents.

"Sydney, this is Maggie." the voice on the other end was deceivingly youthful.

"Hi, Maggie. Is something wrong?"

"I realize this is an inopportune time, but the boys and I are mighty worried about Brett."

"She's not home?"

"No. She was going to lock up for Jack. She's been doing it for years, and she's always come right home in a cab. If she had been detained for any reason, she would have called. It's just not like Brett to not come home like this. Something's wrong; I can feel it."

"I'll go right over. Maggie – what time is it?"

"Five a.m. She should have been back by three thirty the latest. The boys called me at four. They know I'm always up. I've called and called, but no one's answering the phone at the club."

"I'm on my way there now. I'll call you from there once I find out what's happened. If you don't hear from me by five-thirty, then, go ahead and call the police – okay?"

"Be careful, Sydney. Don't go alone. Take Ryan with you."

"It'll be quicker if I run over by myself."

"Be careful."

She leaped out of bed, pulled off her nightgown, and put on her jeans, a blue T-shirt, and a grey hooded sweatshirt, pulling the hood over her uncombed hair. She tiptoed out to the hallway, slipped her key into her back pocket, locked the door behind her, and ran the entire length of Waterloo Row to Willow Place. Unlocking the back door and locking it behind her again, she treaded softly on the industrial carpet with her jute and canvas slip-on shoes. Instinctively making her way to the dressing room through the dark, silent basement corridor, she switched on the light. The cheap fluorescent fixture cast a bluish light on Brett's nude, still body.

"Brett! Oh my God, my Brett!" she threw herself down beside her and gathered her up in her arms.

"Sydney..."

"I'm here, sweetheart. It's going to be all right. I'll take care of you." she kissed her face.

"Sydney...I'm so glad you came back."

"I should never have let you close up alone. I'm so sorry." she removed her sweatshirt and wrapped it around Brett.

"Don't be." she murmured softly.

"Lean on me, Brett. I'll take you over to the cot, sweetheart."

Brett moaned, extended her clenched fist, and unfurled fernlike fingers to reveal the pearls she had gathered up from the floor.

"Oh, Brett, honey!" Sydney managed to remove them, three at a time and shoved them deep into her jean pockets, "Don't worry. I'll get them fixed for you. They'll be good as new." she placed her hands under Brett's arms to support her, "Just put your weight on me."

She managed to pull her up to her feet and lead her to the cot, both of her arms wound around her. She covered her with the faded floral quilt, and rearranged the sweatshirt over her chest.

"Are you warm enough, sweetheart?"

Brett nodded.

"Was it a burglar, hon?"

Brett shook her head.

"This is my fault. I should never have left you alone."

Brett shook her head emphatically.

"Who did this to you? I'll kill them!" she caught a glimpse of Brett's torn dress and panties on the floor, and shuddered in realization.

"I'll get you some water." she crossed the room to the small fridge in the corner and removed a bottle of Perrier; she pulled a Dixie cup with tiny tulips from the wall dispenser and filled it, "Hon, you need to get to the hospital."

Supporting Brett's back, she held the cup to her lips. She then rummaged through the vanity drawers for spare panties in an empty tampon box behind the bag of cotton balls. She pulled back the covers to slip them on her without moving her. From the wall hook, she removed a white cotton button-front sundress, and a navy blue trench coat. She dressed her swiftly, with her sweatshirt over the dress for additional warmth. She brushed her hair and pulled it back into a loose ponytail.

"Don't call the authorities." Brett finally spoke.

"Is there anyone you trust that I can call to give us a ride to the hospital?"

"Chuck."

"I'll call him." she crossed the room to the vanity, and dialled 9 for an outside line as Brett recited Chuck's number.

"Chuck?...This is Sydney. I'm so sorry to wake you up, but Brett's been badly hurt...A burglary at the club...Yes, we're both here...We need you to get Brett to the hospital...Thank you..." she hung up and began dialling Maggie's number from memory, "He's on his way...I promised Maggie I'd let her know how you were. Thank God she called me when you didn't get home...Maggie...I found Brett. She's pretty shaken up. I think there's been a burglary here. Chuck's on his way to drive us to the hospital. I'll keep you posted."

She returned to Brett's side, sat on the cot and stroked her hair.

"Maggie sends her love. Brett, I'm going to be by your side every minute. I'll hold your hand when they examine you. Sweetheart, I know it was no burglary." she kissed her cheek, "I'm going to make him pay. No one's ever going to hurt you again, I promise you. I love you."

They held one another and wept in silence as they waited for Chuck.

Chapter 2/ Charles Delivers

Brett was singing "My Heart Stood Still" with one hand on the piano. Chuck glanced up at her in reassurance. Behind his thick glasses, his grey eyes were misty. Brett was wearing less make-up than usual. Her hair was pulled away from her face with a black velvet hair band. She smiled weakly at the applauding audience. Her eyes sought out Sydney, who was seated at the Manager's table, and remained focused on her for the duration of "Where Can I Go Without You?".

"Any word from the police?" Tony turned to Sydney.

"No."

"If you ask me, it was no random burglary. She knew her attacker, and she's too afraid to reveal his identity."

"Any idea who it might be?" Sydney sipped her martini.

"It could be a crazed fan. Or an employee."

"We have to find him and put him out of commission." she said, "As long as the perpetrator's out there, she's not safe. He could do it again."

"You're right."

"I'm glad you and Chuck were there for her." Jack said, taking the seat on her other side.

"Maggie and Chuck are the only ones who deserve credit. If Maggie hadn't called me, I would never have known something was wrong."

"You were with her to provide moral support. Don't discount that." Jack stroked her arm wistfully.

"Thank you. Chuck was terrific the way he rushed over here and drove us to the hospital. He waited for hours, and took us back to Brett's. He even bought some groceries for her, so I could stay with her the whole time and cook for her."

"Chuck's a good guy. He's no stranger to pain himself. He's been the victim of gay-bashing a number of times since we opened the club. This is a very homophobic town." Jack said.

"I gathered that the moment I stepped off the bus."

"After we first opened, some people boycotted us when they found out we had hired an openly gay piano player. They even tried to torch the place several times. Then, a group of punks followed Chuck one night and assaulted him."

"This is hideous."

"It gets even better." Tony said, "When Jack hired Steve, the singer you replaced, people called this "The Gay Club". They started rumors about Jack and Steve being an item." Tony winked at Jack.

"We were constantly getting threatening calls." Jack continued, "They vandalized the place several times, nearly burnt it to the ground. That drove Steve out. He quit and left town the following week."

"I'm so sorry."

"Chuck tried to quit several times, but Brett managed to convince him to stay every time. She's been his staunch defender all along. He'd move heaven and earth to help her."

"He's a very kind, decent man."

Brett was singing "It Never Entered My Mind".

"She's amazing." Jack nodded toward her, "A consummate professional. I told her she didn't have to return this soon, but she insisted."

"She's a very strong lady." Tony remarked.

"She's keeping this from Shayleigh." Sydney whispered, "She doesn't want to upset her. Shayleigh and Sam don't get to visit too often, because those parents of hers descend on them in

John's Bay every weekend. But she and Brett talk on the phone every day. It must be painful for Shayleigh to be cut off from her only support system, in a city where she doesn't know anyone."

Brett completed her set with "How Deep Is The Ocean?". Before leaving the stage, she embraced Chuck.

"I'll go and see how she is." Sydney excused herself and followed Brett to the dressing room.

"You were terrific out there."

"Hi, hon." she glanced up from the vanity.

"How are you holding up, sweetheart?"

"I'm just fine." she looked lovingly into her eyes.

Sydney stood behind her, rubbing her shoulders, as Brett eyed her reflection in the vanity mirror.

"Please don't tell Tony or Jack!"

"Of course not, Brett. I am so sorry. I feel responsible for this."

"You can't blame yourself."

"But I do."

"Sweetheart, you're not his keeper."

"If I had listened to your warnings and stayed away from him, this wouldn't have happened."

"How could you have known?"

"I want him to pay for what he did to you. He has to be held accountable."

"He's a Horncastle. No one can touch him."

"I'll find someone who can."

"They'll only laugh at us."

"I want him prosecuted."

"In court, the defense will rehash my sexual history and discredit me."

"Your sexual history's no one's business!"

"It will become everyone's business if we pursue this."

"He's counting on us not coming forward out of fear. He thinks he can get away with it scot-free."

"He can and he will."

"Even if he does, he'll at least squirm a little."

"Sweetheart, you have far more to lose than I do. Your parents are tight with the Horncastles. What would this conflict do to their relationship with them?"

"I don't think Warren's their favorite person. They would understand that I need to do the right thing. And, if Aunt Annette and Uncle Donald allow this to come between them and my parents, it would cast a negative light on themselves."

"I don't think they'd care what your parents feel or think. People like them have warped values. They'd sacrifice your parents in a heartbeat, and stand behind Warren, no matter what he's done – even if they despise him. They live by completely different rules than the rest of us. You don't want to mess with them. They'll chew you up and spit you out."

"I can't let them intimidate me. They need to see that some people are not willing to be trampled on."

"Sweetheart, you need to think this through before you make a rash decision."

"My mind's made up. I know there are risks involved, but I'm willing to take them."

"Sweetheart…"

"Come on, let's go up and listen to Jack."

From the stairs, they could hear Jack's cordial, comfortable exchange of anecdotes with his audience. They sat beside an anxious Tony, who searched Brett's face. She clasped his hand. Casting a warm, fraternal smile at Sydney, Jack broke into strains of "Round Midnight", leaving Sydney spellbound.

During the break, Sydney approached Chuck at the bar and tapped him softly on the shoulder.

"Chuck?"

"Yo, Sydney."

"May I talk to you privately?"

"Sure, baby. Let's go around back. Hold that drink, Joe. I'll be back for it."

She followed him to the unlit room behind the stage.

"Chuck, I was wondering if you knew of a lawyer who would be sympathetic to our cause. A Feminist lawyer."

"There are a couple of names that come to mind. There's Marla Bliss, a relatively young lawyer who handles mostly employment related cases involving women: Wrongful dismissal, discrimination, that sort of thing. I don't know her personally or know of anyone else who might know her. From what I hear she's a first class lady. There's one other name I can think of, and, this is someone I have met – socially, mind you – but I've heard wonderful things about. She's been around for a while, and she's known as a renegade: Diane Linton. I think she'd be your best bet in this situation. Why don't you leave it with me? I'll ask around and get back to you."

"Thank you, Chuck."

"No problem. Anything to help out. Keep on trucking, baby."

When she returned to the table, she found Jack in the same seat. Brett and Tony were not there.

"It's a good crowd out there." he spoke awkwardly.

"All your fans are delighted to have you back."

"Celebrity is highly overrated." he said, blinking his eyes, "At the end of the day, we all need to be able to look ourselves in the mirror and feel we can live with what we find…That is not as easy as people imagine."

"Sometimes we can spend years running from the person in the mirror."

"I know all about that." he smiled, "I've never actually removed my running shoes. I wonder what it would be like to kick off my shoes at the end of the day, and settle into an easy chair."

"I still keep a packed suitcase…just in case…You never know when the rug's going to be pulled out from under your feet. The face in the mirror has a way of destroying everything we build up, alienating people from us."

"No matter where we escape to, it follows us, so we're never really free. We try to conceal the guy in the mirror from the ones we love, because when they discover them, they run from us in horror."

"I know that all too well."

"I've never talked about this with anyone before – especially not a woman! Thank you for listening. You really do know what I'm talking about."

"Likewise."

"It's refreshing to have a pal who is a woman."

"Thank you."

Brett and Tony returned, their hands still linked, and resumed their seats.

"Dottie tells me you plan to take some courses at E.C.U. What are you interested in studying?" Jack asked Sydney self-consciously.

"Mainly Sociology and Psychology. Some Philosophy and some English Lit."

"I'm sure you'll do very well. I'm afraid I didn't take any Social Sciences. I only studied Music and Theater Arts." he placed his glass on the table, "Break's over. Any requests?"

"I'd love to hear "Lush Life"." Sydney smiled.

"That one's one of my favorites, too."

Jack returned to the spotlight. In his blue suit and bowtie, he appeared more like a choir boy than an international singing sensation at the threshold of middle age. His eyes remained locked with hers as he sang her request. When he moved on to "Two For The Road", Sydney felt Brett nudging her; Brett gestured with her eyes toward the entrance, where a svelte brunette in a shimmery red mini dress stood assessing her surroundings with icy eyes.

"Miss Young." Johnny O. rushed to her side, "I'll show you to the Manager's table."

"O-oh." Tony squeezed Brett's shoulder.

The brunette glared at the three of them with one raised eyebrow.

"Not with them. Show them to another table. They don't belong here." she looked directly at Sydney.

"But, Miss…" Johnny stammered, blushing profusely, "Mr. Horncastle is the co-owner…"

"In that case, he and his companion can stay, I suppose. Just get rid of the white trash with them."

"We'll all move, Johnny." Tony rose, "It's okay. I see a nice table over there."

They relocated to a nearby table directly facing Jack. Linda whispered to Johnny in a voice clearly audible.

"I don't think the notorious Goldstein woman's that pretty at all. I can't believe she thought she was going to bag Warren. Women like her get used and tossed away. No man wants to be saddled with her sort. What was her first name again?"

"Sydney, Miss."

"What an odd name for a woman. Send a waiter over for my order, will you?"

"Yes, Miss."

She settled into Sydney's former chair, placed her pocketbook on the table, and fixed her gaze on Sydney's face.

"Her Majesty's staring at you so hard, she might freeze that way." Brett whispered.

"She's creepy."

"And dangerous. Stay away from her."

"I'm no threat to her."

"Apparently, she thinks otherwise."

"She has nothing to worry about. Jack only has eyes for her."

"I don't know what he sees in her."

Jack was singing "I'm A Fool To Want You".

"How a propos." Tony winked at them.

Jack's discomfiture was impossible to overlook. He frowned through the entire song, avoiding eye contact with both Sydney and Linda. A decaying crow had settled into Sydney's gut, its wings spread out, poking her with poisoned quills. Its flesh sank deeply, and she sank with it. Thousands of lice emerged from its blood-soaked feathers and were set loose inside her, travelling up to her throat. Sydney could feel the chill of serpentine eyes on her back. She managed to make her way to the backstage room, and back stairs to the dressing room before all went dark...

...Brett was caressing her hair and speaking to her, but she was unable to make out the words. There was a face above hers, fading in and out of view before all went black again.

"Sydney! Sydney, sweetheart, can you hear us?" this was Brett.

"Sydney, are you all right?"

She knew that voice. What was Jack doing there? That infernal crow had come back to life and seemed to have taken up Latin dancing. Hornets were circling its former carcass and were determined to build their nests in her ears. Glancing down at her body, she realized that under the blanket, she appeared to be naked. How had she ended up on the cot without her clothes, and why, she wondered. And, who had undressed her? Who had seen her before the blanket was pulled over her?

"Sweetheart, are you all right?"

"Brett, where are my clothes?"

"You threw up all over them, baby. I had to get them off you."

"Did...anyone else see me naked?"

"Don't worry, hon. I was the first one here. You were decent before they got here."

"They?"

"Jack and Tony."

Then, she caught sight of a flushed Tony in the corner, fidgeting with a Dixie cup. Where was Linda, she wondered, expecting her to burst in any moment to unleash her wrath on her.

"Jack...You need to be with Linda."

"I've sent her home." he leaned closer to her.

"You should go and be with her."

"Not until I have some reassurance from Dr. Collicott that you'll be all right. He's on his way."

Linda must be fuming, she thought.

"No, please, I'll be fine. There's no need for all the fuss." she attempted to move her legs, to no avail.

Linda must think she's faking this. Her rage and contempt must be growing out of control by now. She needed to keep Jack at arm's length, not allow their warm friendship to blossom, for it was destined to be trampled on and poisoned by Linda.

* * *

Sydney opened the door to find a trim woman in a tweed suit, carrying a briefcase.

"Ms. Goldstein?" she smiled, "I'm Diane Linton."

Her handshake was firm and warm. With her softly layered greying hair, piercing blue eyes and calm demeanor, she was reminiscent of actress Barbara Stanwyck.

"Thank you for coming. Please have a seat."

"I hope you're feeling better." Diane sat on the sofa beside the window, "Charles said you've been in the hospital."

"I'm much better, thank you."

"You've been through an ordeal. Charles has filled me in on a few details. I hope you don't mind."

"Not at all."

"I love this part of town. You have a lovely view of the river."

"It's very nice of you to come to the house."

"I find that the client's home is a more relaxed setting."

Sydney poured tea from the silver tea service on the coffee table. Diane placed the pink English bone china cup and saucer on the side table and placed a slice of the walnut bread Sydney was offering on her matching dessert plate.

"This is delicious." she took a small bite.

"Thank you."

"Charles mentioned that this is a sexual assault case, and that you and your friend have been victimized by the same perpetrator."

"That's right."

"I gather your friend is not here today."

"She had more to lose than I do."

"She's ambivalent, then."

She nodded.

"But you are adamant."

She nodded again, more vigorously.

"First, I'm going to get some facts from you. At this stage, your friend does not need to be present." Diane produced a legal sized notepad and a silver Parker Pen from her briefcase, "Your full name is Sydney with two Ys, Valentina Goldstein. Is that right?"

"Yes."

"You're a singer – a chanteuse." she smiled, writing swiftly, "I love jazz. I'm ashamed to admit I haven't been out to Chandler's, or anywhere else, for that matter. Now that I've met you, I have no excuse. The perpetrator...Is it a colleague? Customer at the club? Is it a work-related situation?"

"No, no, nothing like that. But when I tell you who it is, I'll understand if you refuse to take the case."

"Why? You've got me curious now."

"It's Warren Horncastle."

The words hung heavy in the air.

"Wow."

"It gets worse."

"I'm all ears."

"I dated him. At one time, I was…intimate with him."

"Were you still dating when the assault occurred?"

"No. We had pretty well ended things in early fall. He assaulted me just before Christmas."

"Lovely."

"My friend was assaulted three weeks ago."

"The Horncastles live next door, don't they?"

"They also own this house. My parents rent from them. Annette Horncastle is my mother's sister."

"Pretty sticky situation." she frowned, "So, we're up against the Crown Prince. He has quite the reputation as a rogue."

"Do you think it's best to forget the whole thing?"

"Sydney, in the eyes of the law, we are all equal. Being a Horncastle does not provide immunity from the law. He's held up to the same standards as a homeless man in the same predicament, and must be held every bit as accountable for his actions."

"I didn't think any lawyer would accept a case that requires taking on the Horncastle Empire."

"I'm not any lawyer. I'm a Feminist lawyer. I am not afraid to take on the establishment. That's what you asked Charles to find. Did you expect less?"

"I thought I was asking for too much, being unrealistic."

"You weren't. You've been traumatized and victimized. You deserve your day in court. You deserve to be compensated for your pain and loss."

"That's precisely what I had hoped for."

"And that's precisely what you shall have. Charles delivers." she winked.

"Thank you."

“My pleasure.”

“You might be wondering why I waited this long to come forward. I didn’t think anyone would recognize it as rape, since I had been dating him.”

“Unfortunately, those attitudes are still out there.”

“I told myself no jury would ever find him guilty.”

“We are going to be scrupulous in selecting jurors. Young, well-informed women must be well-represented. This is an ultra-conservative town. It’ll be a challenge. If we can keep the religious zealots and the businessmen out, it’ll level the playing field a bit. Perhaps we can tap into the university community. We need as liberal a group as the population allows. We don’t want people with archaic attitudes who blame the victims. Rape is about power, not sex. It’s about time people recognized the reality of rape by spouses and lovers. Whether or not you’ve had relations with someone in the past, it does not mean he has the right to force sex on you when you say “no”. It’s an expression of dominance, not desire. “No” means “no”.”

“I hope people will be less sympathetic to him now that he’s done the same thing to my friend.”

“Did your friend ever date him at any time?”

“No. They were sworn enemies.”

“That would certainly shed a different light on it for the jury.”

“She was always warning me to stay away from him, but I didn’t listen. I was a total idiot. I brought this upon both of us.”

“No self-recrimination. The defense lawyer will be doing plenty of that, so you need not help the opposition.”

“Thank you.”

“What is your friend’s name, Sydney?”

“Bernadette Morrow. But everyone calls her Brett.”

"So, Brett Morrow is the friend you've been talking about." Diane smiled, "I've always wondered if Brett was short for another name. Sydney, I know this is going to be painful, but I'm afraid I'll have to ask you to rehash the events of the evening of your assault."

"I'm ready."

"Take as long as you need. If you don't mind, I'm going to make a tape. It's completely confidential – for my personal use only."

"I don't mind."

Diane reached into her briefcase and produced a tape recorder; she inspected it and insured a blank tape was set up, "Where can I plug this in?"

Sydney pointed out the outlet where the table lamp was plugged in, and moved the lamp to one side to make room for the tape recorder. Diane set it up and began recording, settling back with her pad and pen.

"I'm going to continue making notes, as well. Sydney Goldstein interview." she spoke into the microphone before handing it to her.

"...It was the afternoon of December 14'th...I was working at my family's store, Goldstein's Music Shop. Warren Horncastle came in and tried to be cozy with me, as though we were still seeing each other."

"What was your reaction?"

"I was quite surprised. We had not been together since late summer."

"Who had been the one to initiate the break-up?"

"Warren. He had distanced himself from me by early fall. He appeared to have lost interest in me."

"Was the relationship exclusive during the period of the three months you dated?"

"No. We had never been a couple in the traditional sense. Warren was not willing to commit to a monogamous long-term relationship. Must sound sordid."

"This is the seventies. On the evening in question, what transpired after he came into your place of work?"

"I told him I was working. He said he'd return at closing time and we'd go out to dinner. Then he left."

"How was his manner? Was he charming?"

"No. He was ordering me around and making sarcastic remarks. He wouldn't take "no" for an answer. I did not actually agree to the date, but he said it was not my place to decide whether or not we would see one another."

"What happened next?"

"He returned a little before closing time. He said he had decided we were not going out, but having sexual relations in the back room of the store, instead. I told him it was not a good idea. He became very angry and ordered me to the back room. The more I tried to reason with him, the more incensed he became. I kept pleading with him to stop, but he became more and more violent. He was unable to penetrate me vaginally, so he penetrated me anally…He then threw me across the room…I fell and started hemorrhaging…I begged him to get me medical help, but he refused."

"How did you receive medical attention?"

"I crawled on my hands and knees to get to the phone."

"Sydney, what you've described is a brutal attack – a heinous violation of your trust…When the paramedics arrived, what did you tell them?"

"That an intruder had forced his way into the store, demanding cash, and a struggle had ensued…I hated to lie, but I was so afraid of him. I told the police it happened so fast, and the lighting was poor, so I didn't get a good look at the intruder. I was terrified they might catch an innocent man and ask me to identify him in a line-up. It broke my heart to see my parents agonizing over my putting up a big fight over a few measly dollars in the till. There wasn't much money in the store. Greeney – Grace Greene – had done the bank deposits earlier that day."

"How did you explain the sexual assault?"

"I didn't. I led them to believe the two were not related. They concluded consensual sexual activity had taken place before the struggle with the intruder."

Diane shut her eyes and shook her head.

"This is going to hurt the case, isn't it? They're going to think, if I lied about that, I cannot be trusted to tell the truth about anything else."

"I think we need to emphasize the level of fear you were feeling as your motivation for covering up the truth. The power his family wields, the bond between the Goldsteins and the Horncastles, the innocent people you did not want to see hurt by this...Your aunt and cousin, who might be Horncastles, but are your blood relatives, as well...Your actions were so entrenched in your sense loyalty to your family and your altruism, that any decent human being can relate to that...When and why did you decide to come forward, Sydney?"

"When he did the same thing to my friend, Brett in July. I could not let him get away with doing that to her."

"You put everyone else's needs ahead of your own."

"I feel responsible for what happened to Brett. I should never have kept quiet about him."

"Sydney, what happened to Brett was not your fault. It was Warren's fault."

"Diane, there's something else you need to know."

"Go ahead, Sydney."

"In the fall, after Warren and I were over, my parents and I visited relatives in Toronto. While I was there, I had another indiscretion, I'm afraid. And I ended up pregnant as a result. When Warren raped me, I had a miscarriage."

"Wow." Diane put down her writing pad.

"Did the father of the baby know?"

"No. He has since married his fiancée. It's all very sordid, isn't it?"

Diane shut off her tape recorder and held her face in her hands.

"Who knew about the pregnancy?"

"Only Brett. When I miscarried, Warren found out and believed it was his though I denied it."

"It's going to come out. Perhaps your parents need to hear it from you first."

"I realize that. But the identity of the father must never be revealed. Too many people would be hurt."

"There you go, putting everyone else ahead of yourself again. Were you planning to have the baby?"

"Yes."

"What were you going to tell people about the paternity?"

"Someone I met at a bar in Toronto, a drunken one-night stand, someone whose name I could not remember."

"Do you think anyone would have believed that about you?"

"Probably not."

"Is that what you were planning to tell in court?"

"More or less. Maybe without the bar or the lack of knowledge about his identity. Just that it was someone I met in Toronto."

"You were planning to keep the baby and keep its paternity a secret?"

"Yes. It was the right thing to do."

"Why are you protecting this man?"

"I have no alternative. He was my first cousin. It was incestuous."

Diane was speechless.

"How did Warren react when he found out and believed it was his?" she said when she found her voice.

"He accused me of getting pregnant to trap him into marrying me. I have never wanted to be married to him. Under no circumstances would I ever have agreed to such a thing even if he had wanted it. That would have been a fate worse than death."

"Sydney, the unfortunate truth is that, the other side is still in a position to bring up the sexual history of the complainants. We've got women's groups lobbying for changes, and, some day, such information will be inadmissible in court. But, the reality is, your sexual history and conduct will be dredged up."

"I've only been with three men in my entire life, and I was married to the first one."

"Sydney, I would never pass judgment on you."

"Thank you. Does Brett have to reveal her sexual history in its entirety?"

"Most likely."

"I have no right to drag her into this situation. It's so unfair. Warren must not be allowed to get away with this, but what will all of this do to Brett?"

"She's a fifty year-old divorced mother of three. She could hardly be expected to be a virgin."

"She's been through so much because of him. It's not fair for her to be put through more pain."

"You've been through hell because of him yourself. You've taken a very brave step in coming forward. Your courage is an inspiration for other women. You're an exceptional woman."

"You're very kind. I don't feel too brave. I'm frightened and remorseful."

"No self-recrimination." Diane gathered up her materials and tucked them into her briefcase, "Thank you, Sydney. You did very well. I'm sorry to put you through that. I'll need a statement from Brett, as well. I could meet her here, if she would feel more comfortable. Why don't you speak with her and call me? We'll set something up. It's going to be all right."

"Thank you."

"Call me anytime. My home number's also on my business card. If I'm not there, Gloria, my partner will take a message, and I'll call you as soon as I return." she crossed the room to the foyer.

"Does your business partner have access to all of this?"

"I work alone." she smiled, "Gloria is not my business partner."

Sydney appeared puzzled.

"My life partner."

"Oh! I'm sorry!" she blushed.

"I assumed you'd know since Charles was our contact."

"Please forgive me."

"No, please don't apologize. Your reaction is perfectly understandable and refreshing."

"Thank you."

"It was very nice to meet you, Sydney."

"It was very nice to meet you, too. Thank you for not judging me. You gave me the validation I needed."

"I'm glad I was able to provide that. Be gentle with yourself. Everything's going to be all right." she hugged her, "Call me any time. Take care of yourself."

"I will. You, too."

Diane waved as she walked down the driveway to her car.

* * *

The waif-like teenager peered into Paul's face.

"I'd like to see Dottie, please."

"I'll let her know." he eyed her in disdain.

Another affluent kid with an overpriced, unfashionable wardrobe, he told himself, shaking his head. Fortunately, Miss Dottie had never been like other young ladies of privilege.

"Colette!" he called out to the uniformed young woman emerging from the library, "Is Miss Dottie around?"

"Yes. I'll get her."

"She'll be with you shortly." Paul regarded the young woman.

"Thank you." she removed her white cotton gloves and white straw hat with the decorative blue silk ribbon. Her thick brown hair was cut in a chin-length pageboy. Her photo grey glasses had lightened, revealing aquamarine eyes. Her crisp blue dress with the starched Peter Pan collar and gathered skirt swept her thin ankles. She was wearing low-heeled white Mary Jane shoes, pressing her feet together. Dottie appeared in the opposite end of the corridor and stared in astonishment.

"Hilary?"

"Hi."

"I didn't know you were back."

"We got back yesterday."

And, she had come to visit her this soon. Dottie beamed.

"Do you have time to stay?"

"I've got all afternoon. Mom let me have her car for the whole day."

"Why don't we go up to my room and get caught up? We can come down and have some of Marge's cookies later."

"Sounds good." she followed her up the stairs.

"How was Indonesia?"

"I loved it. I miss it already. I made so many new friends at the American school!" she sat on a white wicker chair.

"The warm climate must have been a welcome change."

"Oh, it was perfect." she spoke in a measured tone.

Dottie remembered their pre-Darnelle days. She and Hilary had shared their innermost thoughts, their hopes and girlish dreams with one another in daily notes, and spent nearly every weekend together. During the entire year Hilary had been across the globe, nary a line had been exchanged between them.

"Are you going to E.C.U. this fall?" Hilary asked.

"Yes, I am."

"So am I. What are you taking?"

"Arts. What about you?"

"Business. Bethany's taking business, too. She's from my Christian Fellowship group. Maybe the three of us can have lunch."

Uncomplicated and well-adjusted, unlike herself, Hilary possessed an exceptional skill at forging friendships.

"Darnelle's taking Science. She's going into Medicine at Memorial after she gets her B.Sc. here. Oh, and she's engaged! She showed me her ring this morning. She and Claude met at some

Science thing last spring. And, Bethany showed me pictures of her trip to Ceylon with the church group. She's really tanned."

Apparently, Darnelle and Bethany had been her earlier visits. She was Hilary's last priority. Her important engagements had been seen to in the morning and earlier afternoon. She was now making her sympathy call. Hilary was only here out of a sense of obligation.

"My best friend April in Indonesia is coming here for Christmas. Her family returned to Kentucky last week. She's going into Pre-Med, too, like Darnelle. She'll be here for two weeks. You'll just love her!"

Hilary lived in a universe that was unfathomable to her.

"I hope you're not hanging around with that awful Clara anymore. I couldn't stand her. Neither could any of my friends. Is she going to E.C.U.?"

"No. Her parents are sending her off to Toronto, to a small college. I can't remember the name."

"Oh, good. I don't know why you ever hung around with that bossy, obnoxious bitch, anyway."

"Would you like to stay for supper, Hil?"

"Oh, no thanks. I'm expected at Darnelle's. Maybe another time. Why don't you join me and Darnelle at my house tomorrow? We're going to have lobster and watch a movie. They're showing "Alice Doesn't Live Here Anymore". Darnelle says it's really good. She saw it with Anna Lise."

"No thanks. I have to babysit for the Caldwells."

"Who are they?"

"New neighbors."

"Too bad."

"Yeah, too bad."

She would far rather spend the evening with Peggy, watching "McCloud". Dottie was suddenly tired, and felt a migraine creeping up on her.

"My new cousin's going to take some courses at E.C.U." she declared proudly.

"I got the scoop from Darnelle. She says people are talking about what a slut she is."

"She's not a slut!"

"I'm not saying she is. Other people are. Then, some are saying she's gay, because she's always hugging Brett in public."

"They can't even make up their minds what they think. They're all idiots."

"Never mind. I just thought you should know."

"Thanks." she sighed, "Why don't we go down and watch "Alice"? The series is much better than the movie, Peggy says."

Chapter 3/ The Garden Path

Brett dried her hands on the lime green checkered towel on the wire rack hanging from the cupboard beside the window, and ran to answer the door. The elfin figure with a cascade of auburn curls rendered her speechless.

"Hi, Brett."

"Shayleigh, sweetheart, what are you doing here?"

"I've left Sam."

"Sweetheart, what's happened? Why didn't you call me?"

"I couldn't. It wasn't private. I'm never alone now."

"Come in, hon." she took her beat-up overnight bag, "How did you get here?"

"By bus."

"Shayleigh, sweetness, you'll have to tell me what's happened. I'm very confused."

"I'm so glad you were home."

"So am I." she embraced her and led her into the living room with an arm around her, "You look awfully thin, hon. Are you taking care of yourself?"

"I'm fine, really."

"Tell me, what's going on?" she sat beside her, "You've never indicated before that anything was wrong between you and Sam. What has he done?"

"It's what he hasn't done. He's let his mom move in with us."

"What's this? I don't think I'm hearing right. You didn't just tell me that Lynn moved in with the two of you!"

"You heard right."

"Good Gravy Marie! In your tiny little one-bedroom basement apartment? Whatever for?"

"Those people she claims are living under her cellar are now plotting to kill her in her sleep, so she feels she has to get out of her house."

"She's got rats in her cellar and hears them scavenging around at nights. A house as old and dilapidated as hers is bound to be full of rats."

"Sam and his friend Al crawled around down there with flashlights, but couldn't find any evidence of anyone living there. They covered every inch of that tiny cellar. No one's been there. The trap door leading to the cellar from the pantry is secured from the inside and there's no other way in."

"She's just looking for attention. She's upset her son has his own life now."

"She really believes there are people there. She says they have discs set up that send her electric shocks through her floorboards, and they talk about electrocuting her. They refer to her as "The Goddamn Bitch". She claims there are two men and a woman, and they have sex all the time."

"The woman's off her rocker!"

"Her doctor thinks it's all a joke."

"It's no joke. She's trying to break up your marriage! She's already driven you out of your own apartment."

"Sam says she's always had these delusions."

"This needs to stop right now. She needs a shock all right, not the electric kind, either."

"Her family doctor enjoys listening to her stories. No doubt, the kinky sexual content makes her a very popular patient."

"He was negligent in his duties. He can't expect you to be stuck with her every day. You're young. You still haven't tasted life.

This is no way to be initiated into the adult world. You deserve a lot better.”

“There’s nothing any of us can do.”

“I cannot allow her to rob you of your youth! I won’t have it!”

“Brett, there’s nothing we can do. Sam and I tried everything. He gave up and let her have her way.”

“Someone’s got to stop that bitch and that someone’s going to be Yours Truly!” she stormed into the kitchen and began dialing the telephone, “I’ll straighten this all out!”

“Brett, who are you calling?” Shayleigh followed her.

“You’ll see, hon. Hello? I need to speak to Sam Cullen please. This is urgent, so please get him out of class. Thank you.”

Shayleigh beamed.

“Sam? This is Brett. Never mind the how are yous. Do you know that your wife is standing next to me in my kitchen right now? Do you even know what goes on in your own household, son? What do you plan to do about Mama Bird? She can’t sleep in your apartment…Well, then, you’ll need to find her alternate living arrangements and some medical intervention. This is not fair to Shayleigh. I know it’s your mother, and she’s made sacrifices for you in the past, but she can’t expect you to be tied to her for the rest of your life. You can’t sacrifice your marriage. Your wife needs to come first…You bet she’s upset. Her home’s been invaded, her privacy violated, her peace of mind destroyed, her marriage is hanging by a thread. May I make a few suggestions, son? First, you look for an affordable apartment for your mother in a secure building with a live-in superintendent. You help her sell excess furniture, or donate it, and put her house on the market. In the meantime, see if there’s a friend or relative who’ll put her up for a little while, or stay with her. But she has to be out of your place today. Tell her it violates your lease to have another person staying there. Most buildings like yours have strict rules about that. She has to tough it out with her imaginary friends for a while. There’s no alternative. Be firm. Get her out and don’t let her back in.

Okay? I'll call you back tonight at ten. She'd better be gone by then. For good. Good luck, son."

"Brett, you're amazing!" Shayleigh flung her arms around her, "I don't know what I'd ever do without you!"

"You know I'd do anything for you, sweetheart." Brett held her face in her hands.

"I'd do anything for you, too, Brett."

"Baby doll, do you mind bunking with me? Keir took your room."

"I'm sorry I'm putting you out like this."

"Not at all, hon. I have a double bed and a big closet. As long as you don't mind."

"Mind? It would be like having a real mom – something I wouldn't know anything about."

"It's never too late to have a mom." she pressed her close to her, "It's never too late to be Mommy's little girl."

*   *   *

Her heart in her mouth, Brett groped for the lamp on her bedside table. The clock radio was flashing two-sixteen like a red neon sign over a sleazy storefront. She turned on the light and reached for the receiver. Something had to be wrong with Laurie! At this hour, it could only be Laurie.

"Hello, Laurie?"

"No, it's not Laurie. You can't even keep track of your own children!"

"Hello, Emerald." Brett winked at Shayleigh, who, by this time was awake and rubbing her eyes.

"What is my Leigh doing at your place? I woke up a little while ago with a very bad feeling. I phoned her place in John's Bay. Sam told me she was with you. Why wasn't I told? I'm her mother."

"Sometimes we need a friend to talk to."

"She belongs here with us. We're her parents. If she's having a problem, she needs to be with me."

"She and Sam are working out their problems. She's going back home as soon as Sam tends to some business."

"I'm sending Henry over there right now to collect her. I don't want her in that den of inequity."

"She's resting now. Why don't you just let her be?"

"You've shanghaied my daughter!"

"This is where she chose to come. We'll talk tomorrow when we're all more clear-headed. Why don't you go back to sleep?"

"How can I sleep when my daughter's upset and I can't comfort her?"

"She's fine. It's all worked out. She'll tell you all about it tomorrow."

"Henry'll collect her first thing in the morning."

"Good night, Emerald." she hung up, "Good grief."

Keir and Toby, who had been awakened by the telephone were standing at the door, yawning.

"What's going on, guys?"

"I'm sorry. It's my mom." Shayleigh apologized.

"Your mom needs to mellow out." Toby said.

"She needs some acid, man." Keir said.

"She's a head-banger." Toby rubbed his eyes.

"I've disrupted your lives, deprived you of your sleep. I'm sorry."

"No, you haven't. On the nights I'm working, I don't even get back until now – don't you remember, hon? You're the one who made it possible all those years for me to work at a terrific job by staying with the boys when they were young, supervising their homework, putting them to sleep. It's because of you, I had peace of mind, knowing I'd come home to a warm, safe house full of peacefully sleeping children."

"Yeah, you let us watch "Police Woman" and "Kojak" on Friday nights! It was cool!" Toby smiled.

"This is the least we can do now, hon." Brett kissed her cheek.

"Thank you guys. You're the best."

"You're family. Your mom's not fit to be family." Toby said, changing his voice to a falsetto, "Oh, Leigh, you're such a rotten kid! I changed your poopy diapers when you were a baby and this is the thanks I get! You live with that trolley and her ragamuffin boys! You never call, never ask about my blood pressure! What have I ever done to deserve such a bad daughter! It's such a dark, dark night of my soul! Other people's children do so much stuff! They're not lazy like you. They have big fancy jobs."

"You've got her act bang on!" Brett said, amidst laughter.

"It's not trolley, you Dufus!" Keir hit him on the head, "It's trollop!"

"What does it mean? That's what she always calls Mom when she comes here."

"It's a horrible thing to say, and she has no right to say it." Shayleigh said solemnly.

"Why don't we all go back to sleep, guys?" Brett suggested.

The boys kissed both of them on the cheek and bade them good night. Shayleigh snuggled closer to Brett and shut her eyes. Before long, she was asleep.

$$* \quad * \quad *$$

"Remember, hon." Brett pulled her closer, "That bank account must remain in your name only. It's your rainy day fund, in case you need to get away in a hurry. Don't let anyone know about it, and don't loan any money to anyone. Don't use it as household money. It's for emergencies."

"Of course. Thank you, Brett. You've been incredible."

"It's the sort of thing parents do for their children. If Sam doesn't grow up and start treating you right, you can strike out on your own. You don't have to feel trapped or destitute. You have your own money."

"All we do is fight now. He says the most insensitive things to me. Then, I feel hurt and say things to him."

"He needs to grow up. I hope he does. But, remember, sweetheart, you are not alone. I'm always here for you. I love you very much."

"Brett, I love you so much."

They embraced tearfully.

"Thank you for driving me back to John's Bay, Tony. I'm sorry to impose." Shayleigh leaned into the car.

"No problem, Shayleigh. You didn't ask. I offered. Take care."

"I'll wait here till you get in the security door, sweetheart." Brett watched her unlock the door and wave from the lobby.

"Sam's a fool." she said to Tony as he made a U turn to drive out of the cul-de-sac.

"He's a good man. Give him a chance. He would never intentionally hurt her."

"He needs to start treating her with respect and affection. She's emotionally starved in that marriage."

"He'll come around. You just have to keep the faith and hope for the best."

"Hope for the best." she sighed, casting one final glance at the yellow apartment building with the amber and orange frosted glass panels on each side of the security door.

Chapter 4/ November Wind

Brett drank slowly from the crystal water goblet and inhaled deeply.

"Sweetheart, I'm so nervous, I feel like I'm going to have a heart attack!" she leaned against the refrigerator, shifting her weight to her right foot.

"It's going to be all right; it really is." Sydney reassured her, "Diane is very nice. She'll make you feel comfortable right away."

"I could really use a stiff drink right now."

"We both need our wits about us for this. Afterwards, we can go out to "Jim's" and get a drink."

"I know, sweetheart." she stroked the re-strung string of pearls around her neck, "I've got my lucky pearls back. That son of a bitch might have taken away my dignity that night, but there was no way I was going to let him rob me of this treasure."

"There's the doorbell" Sydney said, clasping her hand reassuringly.

Brett stood behind Sydney until she was introduced to Diane.

"I'm very pleased to meet you, Brett." Diane extended her hand.

"It was very kind of you to meet me here."

"My pleasure. Why don't we all sit down?" she strode with confident steps and resumed the seat she had taken on her former visit.

Brett tentatively sat on the edge of the Queen Anne chair farthest from Diane and near the doorway. Sydney poured tea and served cucumber sandwiches before seating herself on an ottoman by Brett's feet.

"There's nothing to worry about, Brett." Diane reassured her, "I've already taken down Sydney's statement and gathered some general information from her. All I need from you is your account of the events of July 11, 1977, the night Warren assaulted you."

"July 11ᵗʰ… George Gershwin died on that day, forty years ago." Brett murmured.

"It's okay, honey." Sydney placed a hand on her forearm.

"Take your time, Brett." Diane smiled.

"I might as well get it over with." Brett sighed.

"Do you mind if I tape you? I taped Sydney."

"Sure. Go ahead."

Diane prepared her equipment, handed her the microphone, and motioned to her to start.

"…I was closing up Chandler's Lounge in the early hours of the morning of July 11ᵗʰ, 1977. Jackson Chandler, the owner had asked me to, as he had on numerous occasions before, when he had an engagement, or went on tour, and the co-owner Anthony Horncastle was also unavailable. On that night, I had just finished checking things and turning out the lights, and was about to call a cab and set the alarm when I thought I heard footsteps behind me. I thought Jack had returned to retrieve something he had forgotten. The front door upstairs was locked, so there was no way for anyone to get in…It turned out to be Warren Horncastle…He must have been hiding at closing time and waiting to catch me alone."

"Did he know you were the one locking up?"

"He could have easily overheard Jack asking me to do it earlier when we were upstairs. He must have been at the club that night."

"Did you see him close to your table, or anywhere else earlier?"

"The strange thing is, I didn't. The only one snooping around our table that night was Linda What's-Her-Face, Jack's girlfriend. She kept getting in my face all night."

"I remember her buzzing around earlier too." Sydney remarked.

"Brett, when you came upon Warren Horncastle in the hallway, how did you feel?"

"Shocked, initially."

"Were you afraid?"

"No. I didn't realize he meant any real harm. I thought he wanted to start another argument with me."

"Was that something he did often?"

"Very often."

"Prior to the night in question, had the two of you always been antagonistic toward one another?"

"From the beginning."

"What was the reason you did not get along?"

"He needled me constantly about not being good enough for Tony."

"That is Tony Horncastle, is that right?"

"Yes. Warren's his uncle."

"This antagonism was an ongoing thing, then."

"It had been going on for years. He was an arrogant, condescending jerk."

"Did you, at any time, feel physically threatened or intimidated by him before that night?"

"No."

"So, you had no reason to consider him a physical threat when the two of you crossed paths that night?"

"No."

"What transpired after you found him at the club after hours?"

"He was in a frenzy. He blamed me for the break-up of his relationship with Sydney. He said I was going to get what was coming to me."

"What did you do?"

"I tried to reason with him. I thought I could calm him down, but he was totally out of control."

"What happened next?"

"He forced me back into the dressing room…He ripped my clothes, knocked me about, kicked me, punched me…He tried to choke me. I blacked out. I don't know how long I was on that floor before Sydney found me."

"I'm sorry to have to make you relive that horrendous experience, Brett. Thank you." Diane said. "Do you have any questions?"

Sydney squeezed Brett's hand.

"If my sexual history's going to be fodder for the media, why isn't his? Isn't it just as relevant?"

"It certainly is."

"When his criminal trial comes up, Sydney and I will be the ones on trial."

"Unfortunately, our legal system has a long way to go yet, Brett. There are far too many allowances made for men. That's why we're seeking damages in civil court. It's based on a preponderance of the evidence."

"Do you think we have a case?"

"I think we have a very good case."

"During the trial my past indiscretions are going to be paraded around. He's just going to sit there with that smirk of his, looking lily-white."

"He's hardly lily-white – and people know that."

"The way I've lived my life, people think I deserve to be raped."

"No one deserves to be raped, Brett." Diane frowned, "You were a healthy woman, trying to get your natural needs met the only possible way under the circumstances."

"I liked being married. I enjoyed everything that went with the package. When that was taken away, I was lost. Becoming a bar-hopper was never part of the plan. That blunder came with a high price. I lost the love and respect of my oldest child, my daughter Laurie."

"Kids go through all sorts of phases, and eventually find their way back. You can't blame yourself."

"Laurie wants nothing to do with me."

"It's her loss. Your other children don't feel that way, apparently."

"Warren's going to get off, isn't he?"

"Most likely yes, in the first round. But when we slap the civil suit on him, he won't know what hit him."

Diane rose and crossed the room. She took one of Brett's hands in both of her own and squeezed it gently. The afternoon sun, pouring in the windows on intersecting walls illuminated the intricate pattern of the Turkish rug. As Diane bade her good-byes and the door was closed, Brett flung herself into Sydney's arms, resting her head on her shoulder. They stood entwined, bathed in the light from the semi-circle of glass over the door.

* * *

The porch light cast abstract shadows in the unlit foyer when the heavy wooden door was opened and greeted them with a creak. She pressed the small protruding black circle marked "NO", and the antique copper light fixture on the ceiling burst into a profusion of creamy yellow light in its glass lilies. The black circle was now level with the switch plate, and the one protruding now was the circle above it marked "FFO" with the Fs upside down. She had always wondered why none of the owners has corrected the faulty installation. Perhaps, they, too, had enjoyed the humor in it, and since it functioned properly, had not deemed it necessary. Before she had the opportunity to hang up her pebble white trench coat on the hall rack, he took it from her. He removed his own navy blue trench coat and hung them up. His cropped dark hair was impeccably groomed, and smelling of a fresh field.

"What would you like to drink, sweetheart?" she switched on the living room light.

"Just club soda, please." he followed her into the room.

A thick brown volume of American plays was on the coffee table, with a cocktail napkin from Chandler's as a bookmark. She poured him a glass of club soda, and herself a glass of Canada Dry ginger ale at the bar. Her russet jersey dress hugged her slender curves.

"How long are the boys staying with Josh?"

"Until next Monday. He's being very nice about this whole thing, spending more time with the boys, so they don't have to stay in this gloomy place and watch their mother disintegrate."

"You're holding up wonderfully." he took his drink from her and placed it on a coaster on the coffee table.

"Tony, I'm so afraid..." she hunched her shoulders forward, "You hate me for coming forward, don't you?"

"I hate him for what he's done to you. I hope he gets everything he deserves."

"Thank you." she whispered.

"I'll be by your side through this all the way." he pulled her close, "I'll never let him or anyone else hurt you again...I love you very much, Brett Morrow."

"And I, you. I thought you'd never feel the same way about me again. I thought we were over."

"Nothing in the world could ever come between us."

Her hand clasped over his tightly, she nudged him to his feet and led him to the stairs.

"Brett, are you sure? Do you think you're ready?"

She silenced him with a long, sultry kiss.

"I need to be with you; I need to feel alive, Tony."

Under his touch, her fears dissolved into the warm air. Enclosed in his rapture, she acquiesced to the deep tremors of his body, lulled by his ever-familiar rhythm. The well-known curve of his neck, the mole on his left upper arm peeking out at her, the tufts of hair curling on his smooth shoulders, the warm fur of his chest...all the things she held so dear.

She collapsed on top of him in a torrent of tears. He pulled her down beside him and encircled her with a fuzzy arm. Her thoughts travelled to Sydney: She did not have a supportive partner like Tony to keep her anchored. She had no one to cherish her.

Sydney had never tasted real love with a man she could trust and depend on. For every woman like herself who enjoyed a lush life, there was a shy, lonely Sydney, inexplicably spurned by men, living in exile. When she squirmed, Tony peered into her dark eyes.

"What's wrong?"

"I have to pee." she said, untangling her long, slender legs from his.

He patted her small rump as she scrambled to her feet with the unsteadiness of a young fawn. She did not cover herself with a robe, but started down the hall nude, her marble white skin clearly visible in the dark.

"Don't be too long!" he called out.

In the bathroom, she turned on the cold water tap, placed a towel on the fuzzy jade green toilet seat cover, and sat with her elbows resting on her knees. Tony's allegiance to her would further alienate him from his own flesh and blood. How would she ever be able to live with herself? Then, there was Sydney. What would the repercussions from the courtroom drama do to Sydney's family? Had Sydney thought this out properly, or was she driven purely by her friendship for her, regardless of the cost to herself? Was it, then ethical for her to accept Sydney's and Tony's altruism? Did she deserve such love?

"Brett, honey, are you all right?" Tony was knocking on the door, "You've been in there an awfully long time."

"Come on in, hon." she wiped her tears with toilet paper.

"Brett, sweetheart!" he fell to his knees before her.

"I can't do this to you."

"We've been through this before."

"Don't be noble, Tony. Noble men end up becoming sacrificial lambs. I care too much about you to be that selfish. I have no right to be with you. Please...Please don't say anything...I'm not strong enough to do the right thing and let you go...I need you to help me...Please...Just walk away from me and don't turn back."

"I could never walk away from you."

"What are we going to do, Tony?"

"Just love each other. Our love is strong enough to get us through everything."

"I told you I was a weak woman." she held his face in her hands.

"Come back to bed." he helped her to her feet and kissed her fervently.

Outside, the rain was falling on the pavement and tapping on the small bathroom window. He took her hand, turned off the light, and led her back to the room.

*　*　*

The silver maples lining the path past the rolling lawns were under assault from the bitter November wind, an all too predictable and familiar occurrence in Beavertown. The long, flimsy windows of the ancient building rattled in terror. Designed in South Carolina, the older buildings on the campus, particularly those designated to the Faculty of Arts, were bone-chilling in winter and sizzled in summer. On November days, the wind had a free reign to wreak havoc on the campus.

"Like, if you do stuff, man, stuff you shouldn't do, like, but you don't care 'cuz you're screwed up...So, like, you do it, and like, you can't remember what you did 'cuz you don't want to go crazy...But you feel like you're going crazy, man." a youthful male voice was speaking at the back of the room.

"Sounds like you're already crazy!" voices resounded and laughter filled the room.

"What do you think Mr. Miller here is trying to say, class?" the wiry, bespectacled man at the podium addressed the unruly group, "Miss Goldstein?" he turned to her, noticing her raised hand.

"That, as human beings, we are all flawed. And, at times, we make decisions we are not able to live with, so we block them from our conscious memory in order to cope with them, because being constantly reminded of them would be too painful to live with."

"Very astute. Is that what you were trying to say, Mr. Miller?"

"Yeah. She can dig it, man." the young man smirked.

"That's heavy, man." another young man remarked.

"That's all for today, class. See you on Wednesday." the professor returned to his desk to gather his papers, casting a solicitous glance at Sydney, who smiled absently.

"Miss Goldstein," a white-haired man was making his way down the narrow aisle, "Do you think I could order a record album of Rodgers and Hart songs for my daughter?"

"Of course, Mr. Rollins." she smiled, "We have one in stock: "Ella Fitzgerald's Rodgers and Hart Songbook". I can put it aside for you."

"I would be much obliged, Ma'am. I appreciate your help."

"Who's Rodgers and Hart, man?" one young man asked another.

"Must be a new group. Never heard of them."

"It's gotta be old-people music." said another, "Like that Lawrence Elk dude."

"Yeah, the geezer's ready for the boneyard. He's not going to listen to any good stuff."

"Who's Ella Fitzgerald?"

"Somebody's Grandma?"

"Goldstein knows all the fossils. She sings in an old-people's club."

"She works with that foxy chick, Brett Morrow."

"I'd like to get in her pants."

"Her dressing room's got a revolving door. She likes young stuff. Let's catch her act. Maybe we'll get lucky."

"In your dreams! She's not blind!" a jean-clad young woman laughed, "They'd never let you dummies in the door, anyway!"

"Wanna bet?"

"Plug your ears when you get there, man. The music really sucks." another young man said.

"I'm taking my Walkman with my new Pearl Jam tape and keeping my headphones on."

"They'll kick you out, you idiots!" the young woman hit his arm.

Mr. Rollins was engaged in a lengthy conversation with the professor. Sydney walked out of the room and through the smog of youthful pollutants in the hallway, down the three flights of stairs to the cold.

The November air was heavy with humidity. She needed coffee – black coffee. And a retreat into her subterranean sanctuary: The library basement. She wound her scarf tighter around her neck and sprinted up the hill to the Student Union Building. In the coffee shop, orange vinyl booths lined opposite walls. Orange Formica tables and matching plastic chairs were arranged in the center, leaving scant room for navigating one's way. Young men were congregated around a pinball machine against the back wall, which repeated strains of Middle Eastern music. The juke box at the opposite end of the shop was playing Mary McGregor's "Torn Between Two Lovers". The line was long and progressing at snail's pace. A stingingly familiar voice near the front of the line spoke unexpectedly:

"He's out on bail. He'll be with us for Christmas."

In the corner of her eye, Sydney caught a glimpse of a dark ponytail, and kept her head down.

"If he did it, he should pay the price." a model-thin girl with thick, chin-length hair remarked.

"No one knows exactly what happened, Hilary."

"Your uncle doesn't exactly behave like a gentleman."

"I know he's a swinger, but, rape! My dad says it's preposterous! Warren's very popular with women. He doesn't have to resort to rape to get sex. They're always willing."

"Are you saying Sydney and Brett are lying?"

"They…just misunderstood. There was nothing malicious. My family wants to crucify them, but I don't resent them. They didn't understand him. People are always misunderstanding Warren."

"Listen to yourself, Dottie. It doesn't make sense."

"I love him, and I am not going to betray him."

"I thought you cared about Sydney, too."

"I'm not allowed to speak to her, or about her, ever."

"This is stupid."

"Mom says she should've been grateful a popular guy like Warren wanted to sleep with a Plain Jane wallflower like her at all. She says she must be emotionally disturbed to make up this whole rape story. Maybe Sydney is disturbed and unstable. After all, we haven't known her long. She could have all sorts of secrets."

"A lot of people are saying she and Brett are gay man-haters, and concocted this scheme to extort money from your family."

"Aunt Mildred says a floozy like Brett doesn't have the right to refuse sex from anyone. She says she's just a hooker."

"I don't think they have a ghost of a chance. My mom thinks they're stupid to take on your family."

"Dad says Warren's got nothing to worry about. Just a temporary inconvenience. It'll soon blow over, and all our lives will get back to normal."

"Does Sydney's family have to move?"

"No. Dad says they can stay. They'd never find another wheelchair-accessible house, but they're tenants, just like anyone else from now on."

"Don't you miss Aunt Edna?"

"Mom says she's a traitor, just like Sydney." she paid for her coffee and waited for Hilary to do the same.

"Hey, guys, over here!" a blond young man in a Kelly green and navy blue striped polo shirt at a nearby table motioned to them.

"Hi, Howard!" Dottie led Hilary to the table the young man was sharing with a blonde nymphet with Raphaelite curls.

"Isn't that her?" the nymphet pointed out the cowering Sydney.

"Sh-h." the young man silenced her.

"It's weird that your mom and her mom are sisters, and your dad and her dad are best friends from way back."

"Mona!" Hilary chided her.

The juke box was playing "We're All Alone" by a clean-cut newcomer named Boz Scaggs.

"I think those two made it up." Mona said.

"This is all speculation." Howard said, "None of us know what really happened. This is very difficult for Dottie. Her loyalties are divided."

"What're you having?" a thirtyish man with a white cap across the counter was asking, "Hey, lady!"

"I'm sorry." Sydney blushed, "Black coffee to go, please."

She paid for her coffee and fled swiftly. There would be no escape. This would continue to grow and grow around them until it strangled them. She had brought shame and destruction upon her family, and inflicted pain upon innocents like Dottie. Brett's life would be ripped apart – and more lives would be damaged. There was no turning back now.

She located a vacant bench in the basement of the library near the payphone and put down her books. She sat down, removed the plastic cap from her cup and placed her coffee beside her books. There was a steady flow of traffic in and out of the tunnel past the medieval door leading to the Psychology building. She opened her thick Psychology textbook to the page where she had left off in her required reading. She shook her head at the absurdity of the topic: bestiality. It was difficult to take it seriously, let alone study it. She wondered if other professors dwelled as much on the ludicrous, or was it just her luck to be stuck with the only professor who possessed an unhealthy interest in all the paraphilias. A thin, middle-aged woman in a fashionable chevron-striped dress emerged from the tunnel, sat across the aisle from her, and busied herself with organizing her binder. She glanced at Sydney and kept her eyes on her until she met her gaze.

"You, too, huh?"

Sydney gave her a perplexed look.

"Hitting the books again, as my son puts it, at our age." she clarified herself.

Sydney smiled conventionally.

"I'm Celia Emerson, by the way."

"I'm Sydney Goldstein."

"I've heard that name before. I thought it was a man."

"It's also my father's name."

"What a shame they didn't change it to something feminine when they named you after him. Sadie or something like that."

"It's an honor to be named after him."

"What faculty are you in?"

"Arts."

"What's your major?"

"Psychology."

"So is mine. What year are you in?"

"This is my first."

"I'm in my fourth. I plan to get my M.Ed. in Counselling and work with victims of sexual abuse. What are your plans?"

"I'm doing it for personal enrichment – learning for learning's sake."

"So, it's not a career change."

"I did not have the opportunity when I was young, so now that I do, I want to make the most of it."

"I made the decision to do something meaningful with my life once all my kids were grown. I was tired of wasting my intelligence. You know, you look so familiar to me. Do we have any classes together? I do take a first year Spanish class as an elective."

"I don't think so."

"I know I've seen you somewhere. It'll come to me. Is your husband in the military, too? Do you live in Kingswood? I might have met you at one of the functions. My husband's Colonel Emerson."

"I have no ties to the military."

"What does your husband do?"

"I'm not married."

"What do you do, then?"

"I'm a singer at Chandler's. I also work at my family's music shop: Goldstein's."

"Now I know why you look so familiar! Didn't they do a story about you in the newspaper a while back? You're a long-lost heiress. It was an extraordinary story. It all makes sense now. Chandler's is a gay club."

"No, it's not. It's a jazz club."

"Everyone knows it's a gay club. The owner, the pianist, all the singers…There's another woman with a man's name. There was a Stephen chap. Everyone was talking about him and the owner."

"Chandler's is the only classy club in town." she protested icily. "People who start these malicious rumors are jealous."

"The lady doth protest too much." the woman smirked, "Oh, dear, where did the time go? I have a class in a few minutes." she scrambled to her feet, "I don't think I'll have any trouble remembering your name. Sydney's such an odd name for a woman."

Sydney watched the enviably thin figure dissolve into the bowels of the tunnel. She took a tentative sip of her coffee to test it. It was cool enough. She drank the entire cup without pausing for a breath. She rose, gathered her books, and started up the stairs to the main entrance of the library. The rest of her classes for that day were no longer on her agenda. Sydney started her walk downhill in the ashen embrace of November. The wind was biting. Serpentine branches slithered across a metallic sky. Tears froze on her cheeks. Muddy imprints of maple leaves on the concrete sidewalks formed an Oriental carpet pattern under her feet. She wanted to crawl into bed, pull up the covers, and sleep until the nightmare was over.

* * *

Dottie joined Peggy and Howard at the table.

"Are you guys on speaking terms with Sydney at all yet?" Howard asked.

"Not in this lifetime." Dottie fidgeted with a clear glass salt shaker, "Everyone hates her. She messed up all our lives. Dad says the club is losing business. It's near bankruptcy. He doesn't think Goldstein's is thriving, either. Sydney's pulled away from the store altogether, hoping to salvage it, but to no avail."

"It's a mess." Peggy said.

"I wish they'd all stop this foolishness and be friends again." Dottie dug her spoon into her forearm.

"I'm afraid it's too far gone for that." Peggy sighed.

"I just want my old family back. Nothing's ever going to be the same again, is it?"

"Just wait it out." Howard said.

"I'm sorry, guys."

"It's okay. We'd be just as upset if it happened to us."

"I have to get going, guys." Howard rose, "I promised Mona I'd go to her place for supper. See you in class, Dottie. Bye, Peggy."

"Bye, Howard." Dottie waved as he left the coffee shop.

"We might as well get going, too." Peggy stood and pushed her chair in.

"You're right." Dottie followed suit.

Neither one was in the mood for conversation during their long trek home in the icy twilight.

*　*　*

The grass on the green was a muddy yellow. The river wept into its pewter chalice. Dog excrement dotted the path by the shore. She trudged along in the muck, her feet sinking with every step. The dull gunmetal of the abandoned railroad bridge loomed dark and menacing above her. She braced herself for the steep climb along the winding dirt path concealed by overgrown dead bush.

Down the street, Jack drove into the parking lot of Chandler's. He turned off his tape player and unfastened his seatbelt. As he was about to open the door, a bright blue figure floated outside his window and a tired face peered anxiously at him.

"Iris! What's wrong?" he waited for her to move back before opening the door.

"Sir! Sir!" she was shivering in her hand-knitted cardigan, "There's a woman on the old railroad bridge! I think she's going to jump! I was emptying the trash out back, then, I seen 'er. I was about to call the police, but, then I seen you comin' an' come to get you instead."

"You did the right thing, Iris." he peered intently in the direction of the bridge, and was struck by the familiarity of the figure.

"Iris – I'm going to handle this myself if I can. What I want you to do is watch me. If I'm not successful in ten minutes, call the police. If I'm successful, forget this ever happened and tell no one."

"Yes sir." the diminutive woman nodded.

He sped off in his car and parked in a concealed location behind an imposing spruce. He approached the bridge with deliberate, yet stealthy steps, his heart in his mouth. She was in the middle of the bridge, oblivious to his presence, one reddened pantyhose-clad leg suspended over the railing. He crept toward her like a thief, and in one quick swoop, pulled her back firmly. He pressed her to his chest and kissed her hair. She was reduced to a trembling block of ice.

"I was so afraid I was going to lose you." his tears fell on her hair.

She molded herself into him and sobbed uncontrollably.

"It's all right." he stroked her back, "I'm here now."

"You should've let me jump, Jack. Everyone would've been better off without me."

"That is not true. I don't know what I'd ever do without you, Sydney."

"I've hurt so many people."

"No. Warren's the one guilty of that. You've done nothing wrong. I wish I had been here last year, so I could've kept you safe from him."

“I was such an idiot.”

“No. You were vulnerable. There’s nothing wrong with that. I should’ve been here. I should’ve done everything humanly possible to keep him away from you.”

He released her to lift her wind-burnt face to his. Ice had formed on her eyelashes. He cupped her cheeks with his palms.

“I have no right to involve you in this mess, Jack.”

“I’m already involved. We’re in this together.”

“Thank you for saving my life.”

“You saved my life, too.” tears filled his eyes, “I’ll drive you home. With your parents away, you can get the rest you need. I’ll make you some lunch and chamomile tea. I’ll camp out on your sofa tonight and, I won’t take no for an answer.”

He placed an arm around her and led her away. She placed her own arm around his waist over his navy blue duffle coat. She was not willing to give up the fight just yet.

*　*　*

“Where is he? Iris, I asked you a question! Where’s Jack?”

Iris lifted her head from her cleaning cart and stifled a smile.

“Don’t know, Ma’am.”

“He was to meet me here an hour and a half ago. Did he come in at all today?”

“No, Ma’am. Ain’t seen ‘im all day.”

“Is he with that Cyril chick?”

“Don’t know, Ma’am.” she stifled a laugh.

"You know something! Tell me!" she demanded, "Or I'll have you fired!"

"What's the problem here?" Tony approached them.

"This woman's being rude to me! I want her fired." Linda whirled around.

"Calm down, Linda. I'll get you a coffee upstairs. By the way, Jack just called. He's been called away on business. He sends his regrets." he led her away, winking at Iris on his way out.

*   *   *

Perched on a barstool at the Manager's table Brett was cooing deliciously, the slits of her black gown revealing her long, shapely legs.

"Come over here, baby doll."

A young man with a flushed face stumbled up to her to have his tie adjusted with a proper flourish. Gene and The Matchmakers were playing "The Wave".

"Take five." Gene motioned to his orchestra at the end of the number and approached Brett from behind, planting a sloppy kiss on her neck.

"Hello, sweetheart." she glanced up.

He bit her bare shoulder playfully.

"You bring out the animal in me." he growled.

They shared a clandestine laughter.

"Hey, Wayne, get the lady another martini – on me." Gene called the waiter, "I'll have my usual."

"Coming right up, sir."

Sydney smiled to herself. Gene's "usual" was club soda; he never touched alcohol. Noticing her standing tentatively in the corner, Gene patted her on the back and returned to his orchestra. The club was now open for business and tables were becoming populated with gleeful customers in vibrant attire. A young couple stood awkwardly, jaws dropping and eyes wide. The young woman, upon spotting Sydney at the Manager's table, nudged her escort, and they approached her with overt enthusiasm. Hefty in an ill-fitting suit, the young man wore black-rimmed glasses. His companion, in a simple dress, was delicate in appearance like a primrose, with smooth skin, blue eyes, and frothy brown hair.

"Hi, Sydney." he flashed a wide grin, "We wanted to check out where you worked."

"It's nice to see you."

"What did you get on your term paper?" he continued without awaiting a response, "I got an A+! Dr. Brown said it was the best term paper he had ever read in all the years he has been teaching. He said I'm really going places. He thinks Priscilla's got tremendous talent, too. He's going to help both of us get our work published. Hey, Sydney, can you put in a good word for Priscilla with your boss? She's a really good singer. Looks like you guys could really use the business. Can you get her an audition?"

"You can ask the owner yourself." Brett gestured toward Jack, who had come up the stairs, appearing battle-weary and pale.

The young man made a beeline for Jack, followed by Priscilla.

"He certainly is pushy." Brett rolled her eyes.

"Ed'll go places. He's a go-getter." Sydney said sardonically.

"That little girl knows what side her bread is buttered."

"You're on, Brett." Richard alerted her.

Sydney hugged her for luck and sat back to admire her performance.

"Ladies and gentlemen, the captivating Miss Brett Morrow!" Richard announced.

Brett broke into strains of "Lush Life".

"She's good."

Sydney glanced up to find the woman from the library standing beside her.

"Brett's superb." she responded.

"Does anyone ever sing more chipper and fun songs here? This material's pretty morbid."

"Our material's varied. We sing all jazz standards."

"What do you sing?"

"Mainly Gershwin and Kern."

"You Jews all love Gershwin. I can't see you staying in business for long unless you start incorporating more contemporary music into your repertoire. No one likes jazz anymore."

"Contemporary clubs are a dime a dozen. We offer something unique."

"Music for insomniacs." she strutted to the back of the lounge where her trim, grey-haired husband awaited with two drinks.

At a nearby table, she recognized Victor, a mature student from the same Canadian Lit class as the dynamic duo. He was a balding, retired man with bifocals and a protruding abdomen which appeared seven months pregnant. Victor stealthily approached the table where Priscilla was now sitting alone, while Ed was off wheeling and dealing. A brief conversation ensued, resulting in Victor seating himself beside the pretty Irish lass, and ordering her a fruity cocktail with an orange umbrella and maraschino cherries attached to a swizzle stick. Priscilla batted her long, curly eyelashes at him and listened intently to his chatter. Becoming aware of Sydney's scrutinizing glance, the pregnant man glared menacingly at her. She looked away. A slender and beautiful woman dressed with French flair entered the club and selected a table providing the best view of Brett. Sydney wondered if she was a reporter. Another lone female came in with tentative steps and followed Johnny like an obedient pet, smiling appreciatively as he seated her in the back. Free drinks were supplied to this unassuming woman with the horn-rimmed glasses and fine, straight chin-length hair. The stylish woman with the long raven locks ordered one scotch after another, her eyes transfixed on Brett. She produced a small notepad from her patent leather pocketbook, wrote something, folded it, and beckoned Johnny to her table. Handing him the note and a five-dollar bill, she whispered to him. He nodded obediently. Ed returned to his table to find it invaded by the pregnant Victor. He sat on the other side of Priscilla, undaunted by the competition. Perhaps, it was total oblivion, in the face of the aging Casanova's motives. Johnny, appearing flustered, approached her with the note.

"Sydney, could you do me a favor?"

"Sure, Johnny."

"Do you mind giving this to Brett?"

"Of course." she took it, aware of the Chanel #5 wafting from it.

"Thanks a bunch."

Brett concluded her set with "How High The Moon", and blowing kisses at her audience, vanished behind the curtain. Gene and The Matchmakers began playing "Ebb Tide". Nearby, Ed had accosted Jack once more and his tone was loud enough to be heard.

"I have some background in P.R., Mr. Chandler. This club could use a more contemporary image to appeal to a younger crowd. The only people who know this retro stuff are middle-aged or senior citizens. You and the lady named Brett are undoubtedly superb, but you could also use a younger singer – one who sings more popular music."

"It's very kind of you to offer your expertise, but this is a jazz club. If people want popular music, there are other venues they can seek out."

"Some younger, good-looking singers could not hurt."

"We have a young singer named Danny who draws the younger set."

"What about a young female singer? You need to draw younger men. They are the ones with the largest disposable incomes, your best paying customers. I don't think Sydney has the right image. She's looking kind of haggard. My girlfriend, Priscilla is young and pretty, and talented. She would be an asset to your business."

"I have no doubt she would. They're hiring young singers next door at the Beaver Room."

"Please let her audition for you, Mr. Chandler. You won't regret it."

"We have no openings, Mr..."

"Call me Ed."

"We have no openings, Ed."

"If you could get rid of some of the deadwood around here, an opening would become available."

"There is no deadwood at Chandler's. I suggest you take your promising protégé next door. Excuse me." he walked away.

Ed returned to his table to collect his paramour, to find, much to his horror, she and the pregnant man had vacated the premises, but not before running up a hefty bar bill left for him to pay.

Brett joined Sydney at the Manager's table with a martini in her hand.

"Serves him right." she gestured toward Ed.

"My friend Sydney will vouch for me." he was telling Mark, his waiter, "We're her guests. She'll cover it."

"We're not aware of any such arrangement, sir." Mark said firmly while Ed continued searching in his wallet.

"Looks like you'll be washing dishes, son." Brett called out, "Roll up your sleeves."

"I'm good for it. I'll bring the rest of the money tomorrow."

"If you leave your girlfriend alone for too long, other men will steal her away from you. You may want to spend more time keeping an eye on your girl and less time stabbing your friends in the back in the future, son."

"That pervert's trying to take advantage of Priscilla's innocence."

"I don't think she put up too much of a fight."

"She didn't know what he was up to. My Priscilla doesn't know the ways of the world."

"She sure is a quick learner, though." Brett winked.

"About this bill, I really think you ought to take this up with Victor. It's not my responsibility."

"Victor's not here. You are. Roll up your sleeves, sonny." Brett said.

"You can take it up with Victor on your own." Mark advised him.

"I can do some free P.R. for the club." Ed argued.

"Just roll up your sleeves."

"I don't know why you're making such a fuss over this."

"Poetic justice." Brett turned to Sydney, "What's that, hon?"

"Oh, it's a note for you. Johnny asked me to give it to you."

Brett opened it up and held it so both of them could read it:

"Brett, Cherie...Would like to know you better. I'm the one at the front table with the red rose on my lapel. Call me. Kisses, Gabriele." a number was posted at the bottom of the paper.

Sydney's heart sank as Brett searched the audience and spotted her admirer. The silent exchange between them made her nauseous. Brett folded the note and tucked it into her pocketbook. Sydney shut her eyes tightly. She wanted to wring Gabriele's skinny neck.

"You're on next, Syd." Richard approached her, "Get your act together."

Jack was on the stage, waiting for her. He slipped an arm around her.

"Ladies and gentlemen, Chandler's presents our very own, the beautiful, irreplaceable Sydney Goldstein!"

He held her hand and sang with her. She wanted to bury herself in his arms and never let go. She never wanted to face the world again. Gabriele was watching them in amusement, unaware of Sydney's contempt for her. Jack's eyes remained on her face during the entire set. They concluded with "You're My World" and slipped away to the basement.

"Brett!" Johnny called out from the back, "Phone call for you."

"It must be the boys. I hope they're okay." she said to Tony and jumped off her barstool, "Hello." she picked up the receiver Johnny handed her.

"Brett Morrow?" a raspy male voice was on the other end.

"Yes. This is Brett Morrow."

"You filthy cunt."

"Who is this?"

"You are going to die." he hung up.

Brett stood trembling. Tony came around the back and held her shoulders.

“Brett, what is it? Are the boys all right?”

She clung to him in silence.

“Brett, who was it?”

“It was a death threat.”

“We’re going to the police!”

“The boys! Good Heavens, I have to call the boys! This could be someone who knows who is near and dear to me!” she began dialing frantically, “Keir, hon! Are you boys okay? No, I’m not checking up on you. I just want to know if you’re okay. I trust you, hon. I know you’re not having a party. Can’t a mom worry about her kids? Keep all the doors locked. Don’t answer the bell for anyone. There’s a rash of burglaries in Sunshine Gardens, and we’re just around the corner. I love you heaps. I’ll be home soon.”

“I’ll take you home right away.” Tony led her to the back, “Don’t bother getting changed.”

Brett opened her pocketbook, removed Gabriele’s note, crumpled it, and tossed it into the waste paper basket. Tony placed his trench coat around her shoulders and slipped her out a side door without being noticed.

Back at the lounge, Gene and his orchestra played on. Gabriele ordered another scotch and attempted to proposition Greeney while Leonard was engaged in conversation with another man at the bar. A bemused Greeney demurely shook her head.

“Revolting.” Celia muttered loud enough to be heard, “I knew this was a gay bar! They can’t fool me. Come on, dear, we’ve seen enough. Let’s go home.”

“Ladies and gentlemen.” Richard announced, “Unfortunately, none of our singers are available to perform. Gene and The Matchmakers will be providing instrumental music for your enjoyment, and the drinks will be half price. The management of Chandler’s is very sorry for the inconvenience.”

Gabriele stormed off, nearly colliding with Celia at the door. Leonard returned to the table with a gin and tonic for

Greeney and a scotch for himself. The woman at the back rose awkwardly and requested that Johnny call her a cab. Ed stormed off to begin his long walk home on his own. Gene and The Matchmakers still played on.

Chapter 5/ Venom Soup

The apartment smelled of moist earth and mushrooms. Sam had put on every light, even on this bright sunny afternoon. It was evident there was a concerted effort to make this dismal cave into a welcoming, comfortable home. Cheery floral drapes and furniture covers in blues and corals concealed the outdated Colonial furniture. The knobby legs of the coffee table and the lamp tables flared out. The tacky maple veneer on the pressboard was the color of diarrhea. The cumbersome sofa and swivel rocker dominated the narrow room. They were shabby cast-offs from Lynn. Metal shelves were meticulously lined with books. The only window in the apartment was in the living room, providing a view of the insects crawling in the grass. The frazzled Sam opened the door and moved aside to welcome them.

"I hope you didn't have trouble finding the place."

"I know this city like the back of my hand." Chuck said.

"Thank you for coming."

"You couldn't keep me away, sweetheart." Brett said, "This place is a lot more private than the one you had before."

"Shayleigh wanted to live in an apartment that was part of a family home. She feels much safer here."

"I don't like apartment buildings, either. You never know what kind of neighbors you're going to have."

"This apartment is much more underground than the last two. If you step on the carpets barefoot, it feels damp. We get the pollution from the oil refinery here on the East side, too. But it still beats an apartment building. At least, we don't get the pulp mill here."

"Forest Hills is a solid neighborhood." Chuck remarked.

"We have some very nice neighbors."

"How's my precious one? Still feverish?"

Sam nodded. His eyes were puffy, his hair mussed up, his shirt rumpled; he appeared defeated.

"I think I'll get going now." Chuck kissed Brett's cheek, "I have to catch Uncle Phil while he's awake."

"Thank you for bringing me, sweetheart." Brett embraced him, "Give my love to Uncle Phil."

"Call me in Beavertown when you're ready to go home. I'll come and get you."

"Sweetheart, you don't have to come all the way back to John's Bay. I can take the SMT bus."

"We can drive you back." Sam said.

"I won't hear of it. It'll give me a chance to see old Uncle Phil again. He's not getting any younger."

"Thank you, sweetheart. I love you. Take care driving back."

"Thanks, Chuck. Drive carefully."

"Yo." he waved.

Sam deposited Brett's suitcase outside the bedroom door.

"I don't want to put you out, Sam. I can sleep on the couch."

"I think she needs you close by."

"Thank you for filling me in on what's happened. I hope there's something I can do to help."

"Just by being here, you'll help her. You're the only person she feels close to."

"God love her. How's the bladder infection now?"

"The antibiotics are starting to work. She still gets very bad chills in the night."

"I'll go, lie down beside her for a while."

"I'll go out and get us some take-out later when Shayleigh wakes up."

"I can cook something."

"No. You're the guest. I'll order some pizza to be delivered."

"At least, let me pay for it."

"No."

"Let me contribute to the cost."

"No. I won't hear of it. What toppings do you like?"

"Doesn't matter. What do you kids usually get?"

"Mushroom and bacon."

"Sounds good to me."

"I'll order it in at around five. They deliver in fifteen minutes. Would you like some tea or coffee?"

"I'm fine, sweetheart. I'll just go in and see Shayleigh. You look like you've got your hands full with all those papers you're marking."

"Thanks, Brett."

She opened the bedroom door softly and brought her suitcase into the room. She shut the door behind her and tiptoed toward the bed, where only perspiration-soaked auburn hair was visible, falling on the pink pillowcase. Brett stretched out on the other side of the bed, over the burgundy bedspread, placing a hand over the outline of her arm buried under the covers. She listened to the rhythm of her breath, studied the moist glow of her pale skin, her long lashes resting against her cheeks, the half open pout, and fever-blistered white lips. Ensconced in her subterranean nest, Shayleigh slept, battle-worn and wounded. Brett caressed her arm.

...She remembered the stained white-washed walls, the cracks on the ceiling running in erratic paths, the pungent smell of antiseptic...

"Congratulations, Mrs. Kruger. You have a daughter." a young nurse came in, cradling a tiny bundle, "A beautiful, healthy baby girl."

She groggily opened her arms to receive the cherub, inhaled her new-born scent, traced the outline of pink-white cheeks, and caressed her rice-paper skin...Suckling her breast contentedly, the tiny warm life nuzzled and closed her blue eyes. Her soft head was covered with sprouts of blonde hair, downy like a newly-hatched chick's, but with subtle copper strands.

...On the day of their discharge, a dark-haired older nurse handed her the precious bundle in the white lace layette set knitted by her Grandma Blanche. Enclosing her in the safety of her arms, she peeked at the soft face...The strands of hair escaping from the bonnet were black. The skin was darker; there were definite eyebrows, unusual for one so young, and the small button nose was now a large peach nose. She felt lighter. The dark eyes stared vacuously at her.

"This is not Martha Evelyn." she stated firmly.

"Yes, Mrs. Kruger, it is." the nurse retorted.

"I know my own baby. This is not my Martha Evelyn."

"This is your daughter." she repeated curtly.

"There must be some sort of a mistake. This is not my baby."

"Babies change all the time, Mrs. Kruger. Their looks change from one day to the next."

"She's smaller. Her skin looks darker. So does her hair."

"She's lost some weight. She's had diarrhea. They can lose weight very quickly. Her skin might look different, because she's had baby jaundice. It's nothing to worry about."

"Don't you think she ought to remain here a while longer, then?"

"No, Ma'am. The doctor thinks she'll bounce right back."

"Is he certain?"

"Yes, Ma'am. She'll be just fine."

"I'd like to see him, please."

"Of course, Mrs. Kruger."

...It was the same memorized script from every hospital official in the small upstate New York hospital. Doctors discovered a congenital heart defect (supposedly undetected at the maternity hospital), which began their unrelenting battle. Blood tests revealed what she had known in her heart all along: For reasons unknown to her, she had been given another woman's baby. Her frantic inquiries, her banging on doors, screaming at staff members, her team of bulldog lawyers, all yielded no results. The secrets were locked away, and the gate-keepers were more hostile than crocodiles. She swore she would continue to fight for her Martha, despite being rebuffed, ejected by angry guards, and threatened by thugs at every turn. Her resources depleted, she borrowed from every possible source. In the end, dejected and broke, she was forced to face the reality that her daughter had vanished into thin air. She prayed, wherever she was, that she was safe and loved, and they would, some day, be reunited. For now, fate had trusted her with the fragile life of another child in need of her love and nurturing, a child not expected to live into her teens.

And, that love flourished. Their bond was strengthened through each surgery, each brush with death, through arduous hospital stays. She learned to treasure each moment shared with her Marin, as she lovingly nicknamed her, knowing it could be her last. And Marin, that fragile life, bestowed upon her such love, she abandoned the thought that this was not her biological child. Marin had become every bit a part of her heart, as though she had given birth to her. When she called her "Mama" with that trusting, sunny smile, she longed to escape with her to some uncharted place where the Grim Reaper could never find her. She ached with the impending loss of her treasured child, prayed to be taken, as well, for life would not be worth living without Marin. And, every night, she also prayed for her missing daughter...

Shayleigh stirred and sighed. She opened one eye, and stretched with feline movements. When both eyes opened and focused, she broke into a smile.

"Brett!!! What are you doing here?"

"Sam called me. He told me about your bladder infection. I'm here to take care of you." she kissed her forehead.

"Thank you! Do you have any idea how happy I am to see you?"

"Sam was afraid to worry me, so he didn't call me last week at the height of your illness. Had I known you had returned early and sick, I would have come right over, sweetheart." she caressed her moist hair.

"I had no idea a bladder infection could get that bad."

"It can. And I'm grateful you're over the worst of it now. Until Sam called, I thought you were still away with Emerald and Henry. He told me everything. No wonder you got so sick. My poor baby. Can I get you anything? Tea? Soup? Juice?"

"I don't need anything."

"I'll get some juice for you, anyway. You might need to moisten your lips. You need fluids."

"Okay."

"I'll be right back, sweetheart." she kissed her cheek.

In the kitchen, papers were strewn across the brown and white Formica tabletop.

"I'm getting some juice for Shayleigh. She just woke up."

"I'll get it." he attempted to get up, but she gently pushed him down.

"No, you sit. I'll get it." she produced a juice glass with a heart motif and filled it with sweet red fluid, "Those two should be shot by a firing squad. The audacity of them, spiriting her away under false pretenses, locking her up and tormenting her."

"They told her she had inherited some property in New York and had to go and sign some papers."

"You and I are going to talk about this later, sweetheart. We need to protect her." She returned to the bedroom.

"Drink up, sweetheart." she coaxed her, "Cranberry juice is good for you. Just a little sip. Good girl." she placed the empty glass on the night table.

She had arrived with a firm resolve to reveal the truth once informed by Sam about Shayleigh's predicament, however, she was now aware it might place additional strain on Shayleigh. Yet, she had the right to know the truth. She caressed her curls and helped her prop herself up in bed.

"Do you want to talk about it, hon?"

"Why should you listen to my ranting and raving? You must be tired after your trip."

"All I did was sit in Chuck's car and talk his ear off. I'm here for you, now. You've been through an ordeal; you need to get it out of your system. Look what it did to your body! Don't let their venom destroy your mind and soul, too, hon. Then, they will have won. Don't let them. Fight back."

"My entire life has been a lie. They said I was not really their daughter. They said I was not entitled to anything because I was not their own flesh and blood. They locked me up in this old house, berated and starved me. I'm just a nothing – a no one. I have no roots, no family, no identity."

"No, precious, you are a person with your own unique identity, your own heritage. It just doesn't happen to be what you believed."

"I feel cheated. All this time, I was abused and damaged by people who weren't even my real parents. My entire life's been a sham."

"Sweetheart, you would never have known your grandparents, Aunt Della, or Uncle Seth if you had not been raised in the wrong family. Those four have given you a rare love that will remain with you all your life. You got through it all because of them."

"You're right, Brett. I'm sorry. I'm acting like a self-involved brat."

"No, you're not. You've just had a horrible shock. I think you're handling it very well."

"The whole time I was there, it felt like I stepped into a Shirley Jackson novel, a completely surreal world."

"It's all behind you now, sweetheart."

"There are so many questions, so many fears…What if my real parents were relieved not to have gone home with me? What if, they, too, could never love me if they knew me?"

"That would never happen."

"Would I ever be able to find out who they were? I wonder: Did they ever look for me?"

"I'm sure they looked very hard."

"I overheard Mom or whoever she is tell Miss Hazel that, no matter what the other couple did, they wouldn't get very far anyway. Did she mean they conspired with the staff members? How many people were actually in on this deception?"

"We may never find out."

"I wonder what happened to the other baby."

"Shayleigh, darling…There's something you need to know…You have a right to know…I'm sorry I've kept it from you. I had no right."

"Brett, what is it? Does it have anything to do with my real family? Do you know something about their identity?"

"I've known since before your wedding. I was completely torn about whether or not to tell you at the time. You had enough issues on your plate. I was worried it might do more harm than good at that time. I decided to wait until the time was right. You may never speak to me again for keeping it from you this long, but I feel this is the time, now. You are ready to hear it."

"Brett, please tell me! Whatever you know about my real family, I need to hear it! I am not mad at you for keeping it from me."

"Sweetheart, your real parents loved you very much. And continue to love you very much."

"Do you know them?"

"Yes. Only one of them is still with us. Your mother."

"Please tell me."

"On that cold day in January, in 1950, at Saint Raphael's Hospital in upstate New York, there were seven babies born. Three were girls. One girl was named Jean Marie Anderson, born to Marie and Joseph Anderson from Buffalo; one baby girl was Acacia Leigh Wallace, an underweight baby facing an uphill struggle with a defective heart, born to Emerald and Henry Wallace of New York. The third baby girl was Martha Evelyn Kruger, born to Bernadette and Edgar Kruger, also of New York: A blonde little cherub." Brett was choking with tears.

"I'm Marin, aren't I?"

Brett only nodded. Shayleigh threw herself into her arms and buried her face in her chest to stifle her sobs. Brett planted tender kisses on her face and hair.

"I refused to give up searching for you, no matter what. I said a prayer for you each night. I followed every trail until it went cold. All the records had been altered or destroyed. Everyone on staff was tight-lipped and paranoid."

“How did you ever find out?”

“Tony recommended Stan, a great private detective. He tracked down one of the nurses who worked there at the time. She was on her deathbed and wanted to confess, to cleanse her conscience.”

“Was it a straight switch? You’re sure I’m not Jean?”

“She told Stan everything. Emerald went home with Martha Evelyn and I went home with Acacia Leigh.”

“Were you ever able to find out what caused her heart defect?”

“Rhesus incompatibility with Emerald. Acacia Leigh’s blood type was O+ like Henry’s. Emerald’s was B-, so she developed antibodies against her baby. When the mother’s blood type is negative, and the baby’s is positive, the mother develops antibodies against the baby, which destroy the baby’s immune system and do all sorts of damage to all the organs. Many times, babies are stillborn. Sometimes, if it’s the first pregnancy, the baby can be safe, but if it’s the second pregnancy following a miscarriage, the baby is in trouble. Back then, they didn’t know about these things. Now, there are things they can do to prevent this. Do you, by any chance, know if Emerald had another pregnancy?”

“Yes. Less than two years before Acacia Leigh. She had a miscarriage when she was seven months pregnant.”

“Those two were never meant to have children.”

“I’m glad Acacia Leigh had you for a mother. She needed you more at the time. It must have been fate she went home with you. I found you when I needed you most. I didn’t know you were my mom, but I always thought of you as my mom.”

“Are you sure you’re not disappointed to have a hard-drinking lounge singer for a mom? Laurie wants nothing to do with me, and I can’t say that I blame her.”

“I’m not Laurie. I love you. I need you. Brett, you are all the things I want in a mother. I want to be a real daughter to you.”

"You are, sweetheart."

"Brett, how would you feel about me changing my name to Marin? I don't want to diminish the memory of Martha Evelyn."

"It's your rightful name, darling – your true identity – your birthright."

"The name belonged to her during the brief life she had and it is rightfully hers."

"I think it's a lovely tribute that you'd want to honor her memory and carry on her name. She was here for only a short time, but she left her mark in people's hearts. She would be honored to know you want her memory to live on."

"I am not trying to take her place."

"Sweetheart, I know that. And, looking down from heaven at us, she knows that. Maybe she brought us together. She did this for you. You took Emerald's wrath in her place. She wants you to come home, at last."

"I wish I knew more about your – our family."

"I would love to take you and Sam and the boys to Vermont to meet some of the family. My sisters Vera and Mary are there; so are my brothers Joe and Paul, with their families. Paul has two daughters, Lily and Harley. He loves motorcycles, as you can tell. Both girls are married and have young children. Joe had three sons. Two are in university. One is teaching overseas. My sister Joan lives in Rhode Island; Polly's in Maine, and my brother Alf's in Massachusetts. I hope they can join us, too. Joan's daughter Marybeth lives in Connecticut. She's very close to Polly. Both Polly and Alf spoil her, because neither one has children."

"That's a huge family! I can't believe I've got all those aunts, uncles, and cousins!"

"My mother was pretty busy. She had a hard life, God rest her soul. Never had a break. Pretty well raised all eight of us on her own. Dad was no help. He was a hopeless drunk."

"I'm sorry."

"Mom was terrific. There always seemed to be enough food and money for all of us, even some left over for the hobos who came by begging. Mom never turned anyone away."

"I wish I could see all the places you were in as a little girl."

"We'll all take a trip together. The family home and the farm are long gone now. There's a subdivision over it."

"I can't wait for Sam to know all this, to see the look on his face."

"Come on, baby girl. Let's bring him in here and give him the news. I'll go get him."

Shayleigh smiled: Marin. That was her new name. She would gather all of her happy memories from her existence as Shayleigh and lock them away. New memories would be created as Marin. Tonight, she would sleep as soundly as a newborn. As soundly as the newborn once suckling Brett's breast. Then, in the morning, Brett would be there when she awoke.

Chapter 6/ Marin

She was jolted awake by the sound of the train pulling into the station. Her head resting on Brett's shoulder, she inhaled the sweet Oriental scent of her cologne blending with her own natural, moist fragrance. Brett's arm was placed protectively around her. This was the most natural spot for her; it was where she belonged. Outside the window, crumbling houses of the urban core were silhouetted against a dove-colored summer sky. Lights in the windows were like distant television screens.

"Hi, sweetheart." Brett smiled, feeling her stirring.

"Hi, Mom."

"We're in John's Bay." she kissed her hair, "You've been asleep for a long time."

"I'm sorry! I've hurt your shoulder." she bolted upright.

"You could never hurt me, baby girl."

She reached up and kissed Brett's foundation-scented cheek.

"You've been asleep since Bangor."

"Your poor shoulder!"

"You were light as a feather, hon."

"Thank you."

"Sam and the boys are waiting for us inside the station. They got off and collected the luggage before you were fully awake. Sam's calling a cab."

"Mom – thank you. These past three weeks have been the most glorious in my entire life. Everyone was so welcoming."

"They were elated to be reunited with their niece."

"Thank you for wanting me."

"Thank you for accepting me."

They made their way down the narrow aisle single file, with Brett in front, her hand linked with her daughter's behind her. The infamous chill of John's Bay's year-round gales greeted them. The aged harbor city shivered, its weary, rat-infested slums bowing their heads in shame. Sam greeted them by the entrance to the station.

"Our cab's on its way. Keir and Toby are inside with the luggage."

"Are you sure you want us to spend the night at your apartment, Sam? Won't things get pretty crowded for you?"

"Not at all. You ladies take the bedroom. The boys and I can crash in the living room. I borrowed three sleeping bags from the landlord just before we left."

"Are you sure the landlord's family won't mind? My boys are rambunctious."

"They've raised five children. They still have two teenagers at home. I'm sure they're used to normal noise levels. Besides, they know the circumstances."

"I'll treat all of us to pizza for supper tonight. We'll have it delivered. Tomorrow, before the boys and I return to Beavertown, I'll take us all out to a nice Chinese restaurant for a lunch buffet."

"You don't have to do that, Brett."

"It's my pleasure. Call me Mom."

"Mom."

As their taxi pulled up to the curb, the grey-haired driver rolled down his window.

"Are youse the folks who called a cab to go to Forest Hills?"

"Yes. Party of five. We have luggage. I'll be back." Sam opened the back door for the women and ran into the station.

The driver stepped out to open the trunk and waited for Sam and the boys to return with six suitcases. He loaded them efficiently. Sam and Keir sat up front. Toby climbed into the back with his mother and sister.

"Tony must have the paperwork completed, or close to being completed." Brett said, "Soon, you will be Marin legally. Thank you for taking Blanche as your middle name."

"I wish I could have met her. The least I can do is honor her memory."

"She would have been so proud of you."

"Welcome to the family, Marin Blanche." Toby said.

"Marin...I am Marin." she smiled, "Good-bye, Shayleigh. Rest in peace. I buried you."

When she shut her eyes, laughter and birdsong filled her reverie. Aunt Veronica's immaculate blue Victorian house in Vermont was filled with fifteen relatives, brimming with joy. All six bedrooms were occupied: She and Brett occupying one; Sam and the boys in the next one, the one large enough for three twin beds; Aunt Veronica and Aunt Marg in the third; Aunt Joan, Aunt Polly and Cousin Marybeth sharing the enormous master bedroom; Uncle Joe and his wife Marion occupying the fifth room; Uncle Paul and his wife Theresa in the sixth one. Uncle Alf slept in the den downstairs.

Each day was filled with picnics in the country, visits to historic sites and beaches, Lily and Harley's homes, shops, zoos, cookouts in the backyard. Evenings were spent gathered around the grand piano, with Brett leading singalongs. At times, they broke into smaller groups and dispersed to various locations throughout the house and the enormous backyard. The four men shared beer and sports talk on the back porch. Sam and the boys kicked a ball and tackled each other on the rolling lawns. The nine women moved fluidly in and out of random groupings. She was part of a real family. She was accepted and wanted. She finally belonged.

* * *

Dottie stood at the intersection of Regent Street in front of the dark brown post-modern church, waiting for the traffic light to display the green man walking.

"If "Walk" is a green walking man, then, why isn't "Don't Walk" a red man standing still?" she had remarked at the campus coffee shop one afternoon, "A red hand is not the opposite of a green man."

"That's a good one, Dottie!" the others at her table had roared with laughter.

She smiled to herself as she crossed the street. Minette should have been with her now to share the experience of being in university. Minette with the dancing eyes. Never again would she experience the exhilaration of sharing a bond with someone like Minette. No one else understood the pain of being alive, alienated and afraid. Without Minette, there would always be a gaping hole in her heart. Following Minette's death, everyone at school had behaved as though she had never existed. Just like the stiff, frigid Beavertonians they had been raised to become, all had kept silent. No one had cared when she lived and no one cared when she died. Minette had been deemed insignificant by the elite of Beavertown High.

She did not relish the evening Clara had planned for them: Standing outside the houses of all the "cute" boys from their high school days who were home for summer break. Clara still compulsively engaged in this old ritual each time she was in town. Dottie could never remember the names or faces, for all of them were equally repulsive to her. Nevertheless, out of self-preservation she was compelled to keep up the charade of being interested in boys, as well. This necessitated participating in Clara's schemes.

Hilary was the only girl besides herself who did not keep company with young men. But Hilary did not appear troubled by this slight blemish on her otherwise flawless existence. Surrounded by friends from her Christian Fellowship group, being unattached, for Hilary, was out of choice, not necessity. Unlike Dottie, Hilary exuded a serenity known only to the very pious or the very unaware.

Howard was her one true friend – the one kindred spirit – and the only one she had confided in about her hopeless crush on Professor Philip Anderson O'Hurley, the aloof, bespectacled, pipe-smoking History professor.

Her fractured family continued floating through the motions of daily life, exhibiting behavior expected of them in the sanitized sphere of Beavertown elite. No one mentioned Sydney now. Jack seldom visited. Tony worked longer hours and did not come home for dinner. Warren cultivated his aptitude for real estate. Life went on.

*　*　*

The front door was left ajar. Two milk bags were deposited on the worn concrete steps. She gathered them up and called out into the dark interior.

"Mrs. Parker! Mrs. Parker! Are you here?"

No response came. She called out again.

"Who is it? Who's out there?" a frightened little voice came from the back of the house.

"Mrs. Parker, it's me, Sydney! Sydney Goldstein."

"Oh, Sydney, dear!" she emerged from the kitchen, trembling.

"Your front door was open."

"Oh, was it, dear?"

"The milkman had left these on the front steps." she held up the milk bags, "I'll put them away for you."

She proceeded toward the kitchen.

"Isn't this the day Joe's bringing the ice?" Daisy followed her.

"Joe? Ice?"

"For the ice box. He's my iceman."

"You don't need it, Mrs. Parker. Joe doesn't have to bring ice anymore. Your refrigerator works on its own."

"Does it? Well, isn't that clever? What will they think of next? Oil lamps that clean themselves? Today must be the day Fred brings my coal for the furnace, then."

"You don't need coal, either, Mrs. Parker. Your furnace uses oil now."

"Oh, yes. My dear departed husband Alfred bought the new furnace...Won't you have tea, dear?...I must tend to my chicks now."

"Your chicks?"

"Yes. Baby chicks. I'm hatching two dozen baby chicks on my stove. Come and see them, dear. But you must be careful. We don't want to frighten them."

Perplexed, she followed Daisy to the stove, with the oven turned on. Two egg cartons were placed on the two front burners. Sydney turned off the oven and moved the cartons to the counter.

"No, dear. We must keep them warm, you know, or they'll die."

"Mrs. Parker, these chicks can't hatch. They are store-bought eggs."

"Where do you think chicks come from, dear? Eggs! My hens laid them this morning. The fox ate my hens. I have to hatch the chicks myself."

"Mrs. Parker, these eggs can't hatch. They have been refrigerated for some time at the supermarket."

"That is so cruel!" she burst into tears, "How could they do such a thing? They killed my baby chicks!"

"Please let me refrigerate the eggs for you. They were not your baby chicks. There were no hens or baby chicks. You live in the city now."

"I don't like the city."

"Mrs. Parker, your front door should be locked at all times. I know I sound like a meddler, but it's for your own safety. There have been an awful lot of break-ins in Beavertown recently. Please keep it locked and don't open it for anyone you don't know, no matter what, whether they say they're selling something or they need to use your phone to call for help. Please, please be careful."

"My neighbor, Mr. Carruthers had to shoot his horse yesterday. It just broke my heart." her eyes were glazed like a raccoon's.

Sydney's heart sank. She racked her brain for a glimmer of hope.

"Are you here to take care of Lillian, dear?" Daisy turned to Sydney without a sign of recognition, "She's my little sister. Don't let anything happen to her. Papa says it's this late thaw we've had. Poor thing."

"Mrs. Parker, I'm Sydney, your friend and one-time lodger. Remember me? I'd like to stay with you tonight; is that okay?"

She only stared blankly at her.

"Is it all right if I use your phone?"

"Yes, dear. You tell that operator, Sarah, that I'll give her my quince jam recipe if she gives me her red currant jelly recipe."

"Yes. I will."

Once out of Daisy's earshot, she dialed Jack's private number. Her heart leapt in relief when she heard his voice.

"Jack, this is Sydney. I'm at Daisy Carter's house and something is very, very wrong."

"What is it? Is she ill?"

"She might be. Her door was open when I came in. She's talking about people from the past, thinks I'm her sister's nurse. She almost started a fire trying to hatch some eggs in their cartons. I'm terribly worried. It could be Alzheimer's."

"Let me make a few calls and see if I can get a health care agency to send homemakers to stay with her around the clock. Doesn't she have a daughter somewhere? If you can give me her name and number, I'll call her."

"I'll take a peek in her personal address book." she rifled through the drawer where notepads and pens were kept, along with a brown leather-bound notebook, "I've heard her mention her a few times. I don't think they're too close. Her name's Maureen. I think this is it." she paused at one page, "Nickerson: Maureen and Bert. They live in Iowa. I'll give you the number." She read it out slowly.

"Tell that Sarah she owes me that recipe." Daisy called out from the kitchen.

"Jack, I'll have to go. I'm going to be here all night."

"I'll get on the phone to an agency now and see if I can get a worker to relieve you in the morning. I'll be dropping by later."

"Thanks, Jack. I appreciate everything."

"Don't mention it, Sydney."

"I want to see Mama." Daisy emerged from the kitchen, "Why won't they let me see her? Is she very ill?"

"Mrs. Parker, this is 1978."

"That means Mama's one hundred and sixteen now. Where is she? Can you take me to visit her, dear?"

She was losing Daisy. She embraced her tearfully. Yet, still in those eyes was the essence of her being, the unblemished core of her spirit.

Chapter 7/ I Didn't Know What Time It Was

While Gene and his band played, she faded into the dark corridor unnoticed, and slithered down to the dressing room. She was aching in longing for all she held dear: Her parents, her dear friends – Brett, Daisy, Maggie, Shayleigh (now Marin, much to her delight), Greeney – and her dear, precious Dottie, who was already lost to her, working at a job she had dreamed of all her life...Most of all, this deepening connection with Jack...Euphoric, overwhelming, frightening – so frightening. They were all about to be taken away from her. The pain of Jack's loss was settled in her. All of them had been gifts generously endowed by the Powers Above. Why had she been deemed deserving? Perhaps, it had all been a test of her worthiness – and she had failed the test. Miserably.

She had not seen any of this coming. She had never imagined her poor judgment would, some day, end up costing her everything she cherished and destroying the people she loved most. Her mother had lost her sister; her father had lost a lifelong friend. Jack and Tony had been alienated from their family. The damage caused by her unwise choices was irreparable. She could not remain in this town.

Upstairs, Brett was singing "More Than You Know". Brett – her cherished Brett – would remain locked in her heart always. Slowly, she started toward the door. Hearing footsteps behind her, she turned around to find Jack.

"Can we talk in my office?" he asked.

She complied, but declined the drink he offered.

"I wanted to tell you Daisy's going to be all right." he said, "She had been running a fever with the flu and she accidentally took too many sedatives through the day, mistaking them for antibiotics. The bottles looked very similar. That caused her confusion. Her daughter flew here the next day. She's recently retired and she's decided to move here to be close to her. She called me this afternoon to report Daisy's back to her old self now."

"Thank you for everything, Jack. I was so upset when I found her like that, I didn't know what to do."

"I'm glad you called me."

"You're always there for me. You're my angel."

"You're the angel, Sydney."

"Not by a long shot." she laughed nervously.

His arms enclosed her. Chills shot through her. Upstairs, Brett had concluded her set. Gene had gone home early with flu-like symptoms. Recorded music was being piped in throughout the building. Ella Fitzgerald was singing "I Didn't Know What Time It Was".

"No one can sing this song the way she does." she murmured.

"Let's dance." he whispered.

She surrendered to his arms and followed his lead. Quivering under his touch, she longed to dissolve into his skin. He was not wearing cologne. Through the thin fabric of his shirt, she could smell his moist, musky scent. She inhaled deeply. This was the way she wanted to remember him.

The song ended. His eyes were burning through her. His index finger traced the outline of her lips. He kissed her between her eyes. His lips moved lower, brushing the tip of her nose, lingering close. Her heart was thrashing in her ribcage like a captive bird. She could feel his warm breath on her face and the beating of his heart against her.

"Ahem."

This intrusion came upon them, forcing them to pull apart reluctantly. Richard was standing in the doorway.

"Gene cannot come in tomorrow night, boss. He had to go to the hospital tonight. His wife called."

"Thank you, Richard."

"Look, whatever you do in your own time is your business, boss." He walked out, shutting the door behind him.

"I should've locked the door." Jack said, flustered, "I'm sorry about that."

"Please don't be."

"I'll take you home."

Neither one of them spoke in the car. She kept her eyes lowered.

"Thank you, Jack." she murmured when he pulled into her parents' driveway.

"Take care, Sydney." he searched her face.

They exchanged timid smiles. He waited for her to open the front door with her key and turn on the hallway light before he drove away.

*   *   *

"Thank you for switching sets with me, sweetheart." Brett kissed her cheek, "Toby's got that flu that Gene has, and I've got to get home to take care of him."

"Any time, Brett. I hope he feels better."

"Thanks." she blew her a kiss and closed the door behind her.

Sydney smoothed her Bordeaux chiffon gown and reapplied her lipstick. A knock was at the door.

"Sydney, are you decent?"

108

"Yes, I am, Jack."

He stepped tentatively into the dressing room and lingered close to the door.

"Are you all right?"

"I'm fine. You don't have to worry about me. How about you?"

"I didn't sleep a wink last night."

"Neither did I."

"We need to talk about what happened last night. If Richard had not come in when he did, I don't think I would've been able to prevent the inevitable."

"If you'd like me to keep my distance from now on, I understand."

"I don't. I never want to be away from you."

"Neither do I."

"Richard may not show up to interrupt us next time."

"I had never thought of Richard as the morality police before." She smiled.

"What are we going to do, Sydney?"

"I wish I knew the answer, Jack."

"It feels so right, so natural to be with you. You've been my dearest friend for over two years. Now, it's so different. Our friendship has caught fire."

"I only want what is best for you, Jack. I'll do whatever you want."

"All I ask of you is to do what makes you happy."

"Jack, I think it would be best for you and everyone else if I leave town once this trial is over."

"Sydney, you can't. Where would you go?"

"I know you're losing business because of me, but you're too nice to say anything."

"Business is fine. You're the one that matters."

"I can't take advantage of your good nature."

"Let's not discuss any of this now. Not if it means losing you."

"You're better off without me." she said, her voice quivering.

"No. I can never let you go." he met her gaze, "Never."

"I'll stay if you want me to."

He extended his hand to accompany her upstairs. She took the hand he offered and smiled.

*　*　*

"Isn't Loverboy suspicious that you're not going to the club anymore?" Warren inspected his fingernails.

"You're his uncle. You ought to know how thick he is." Linda bent over the bed and ran a fat hairbrush through her waist-length tresses.

"So, have you love birds set the wedding date?"

"He keeps putting it off out of respect for your family. He wants to wait until your trial is over."

"Or maybe he thinks he doesn't need to buy the cow since he's been getting the milk for free." he smirked.

"He hasn't been too interested in my milk lately."

"Maybe he's been getting his supply of milk from another cow. They do spend an awful lot of time together."

"I'm not worried about that mousy little thing." she laughed, shook her hair and climbed back into bed beside him, "I still can't figure out what you ever saw in her."

"You already know. I was investigating her to make sure she wasn't an imposter out to fleece Edna and Sid."

"And, of course, this investigation could not be conducted without taking her to bed."

"That's where I do my best work. You ought to know." he winked.

"You didn't have to keep sleeping with her after that."

"She was easy."

"I hope you're not saying that about me behind my back."

"Linda, you're not easy. You're exciting and enticing."

"Aren't you the charmer?" she stuck her tongue out at him.

"If you're not worried about her, why do you hate her so much?"

"Because I think you're still obsessed with her."

"She didn't mean anything to me. Just an easy lay."

"I'm not buying that. You were with her for months, did things for her – like the time you sent those goons after her friend's grandson to put the fear of God into him. Look how she repaid you. You must feel so betrayed."

"I think you're the one who's obsessed with her. Why do you ask so many questions about her? Why do you talk about her non-stop?"

"Was she any good in bed?"

"Why do you want to know?" he snapped.

"Just curious."

"If you're so curious, why don't you fuck her yourself?"

"I don't swing that way."

"You sound like you do, the way you go on about her. I've had enough. Stop with all these questions."

"Does she swing both ways?"

"I don't know and I don't care, Linda."

"Rumor has it, she and Brett are more than friends. Is that true?"

"I told you: I couldn't care less. Give this a rest. You're getting on my nerves." he bolted out of bed, gathered his clothes from the floor, and stormed out of the bedroom.

*　*　*

Jack descended the dark stairs, unlocked his office, and switched on the fluorescent lights. On the floor, there were envelopes slid under the door by Johnny. He picked them up and placed them in the black metal basket on his desk. A postcard sandwiched between two small envelopes caught his eye. The well-known sight of the "Painted Ladies" of San Francisco graced one side, and an elegant handwriting in turquoise ink, the other.

"Hi, Jack. San Francisco is fabulous. Wish you were here. I think I've finally found a place to settle down. How is Sidney working out? Take care. Miss you. Love, Stephen."

Jack noted the misspelling. He tucked the postcard into the left bottom desk drawer.

"You have to fire that girl, Jack, dear." Aunt Mildred had admonished him a year earlier, "She's trying to destroy our family. Look what she's done to our Warren. Where's your loyalty?"

"I would never do that to her, Aunt Mildred."

"Both you and Anthony have lost your marbles. You're too chummy with her, singing duets with her, from what I hear.

People talk, you know. They've seen the way she makes eyes at you."

Sydney's eyes...Dark, hypnotic, intoxicating...He longed to hold her again, dance with her, and never let go. He was filled with a peculiar yearning he could not fathom. It was unlike anything he had ever felt for another woman. He longed to protect Sydney from harm, keep her safe. Whatever this disconcerting, indescribable bond was between them, it was an integral part of his life, not one he was prepared to part with. There was an intensity, a depth he was unaccustomed to experiencing with women.

He buried his head in his hands. Light footsteps down the hall and up the stairs indicated Sydney was about to begin her set. He waited until she had sufficient time to join Chuck before going upstairs and sitting at the center front table with a more unobstructed view of her than the Manager's table.

Shimmering in her ruby gown, she fixed her gaze on him and broke into strains of the sultry "I Didn't Know What Time It Was". It would be so easy to become lost in the dark intensity of her smouldering eyes. Those eyes, burning into his subconscious, followed him, came upon him at unexpected moments. Were Sydney to walk out of his life, he feared parts of himself, too, would become lost to him permanently. He was aware other men would risk losing their souls for the safety of ignorance and the familiarity of blindness. They would sacrifice her for the comfort of conformity. Most men feared that glimpse into the depths of uncharted territory. Letting her go would mean returning to the numbness that had engulfed his life before. It would mean a fate worse than death. For that, he was not prepared.

* * *

"Peggy, guess what I found out from Tony last night!" Dottie burst in through the kitchen door and deposited her books on the counter.

"Go on, tell me!" Peggy glanced up from the soup she was stirring on the stove.

"Shayleigh is Marin now."

"She's what?"

"Marin."

"What does that mean?"

"That's her real name. She's really Brett's daughter."

"Run this by me again." she turned off the electric burner and covered the saucepan.

"She was switched at birth. Emerald and Henry's baby went home with Brett. That baby had a heart defect and didn't live long."

"This sounds like something right out of a movie."

"It does, doesn't it? Tony's helping her get her name changed legally."

"Some happy news for a change."

"I've got a juicy story, too."

"You've got to tell me."

"It turns out that "The General's Inn" is actually a brothel, not just a flophouse. This guy Lucas from my English class said his friend Trevor from John's Bay came to town to visit his girlfriend Ayesha on the weekend. Her parents are super strict and weird and wouldn't let him stay at their house, so the poor guy decided to rent the most affordable room he could find. There was nothing cheaper than "The General". When he and Ayesha went to get him a room, there was this mean old woman at the desk with a Doberman next to her. She told them no women were allowed upstairs. That's because they provide their own. Then, later, when Trevor told some of his friends about it, they told him it's been like that since 1970. Not only that, Lucas said, but some of the local guys found out these girls from my Junior High home room,

Barbie and Mandi were hookers there and had been, since High School.”

“Wow. I should be shocked, but knowing what a dive that place is, I’m not.”

“Those girls always looked old and jaded.”

“I wonder where they’ll be by forty – if they live that long, that is.”

“It feels creepy to know stuff like this. I nearly puked.”

“We’re living in perilous times, honey. There are more young people losing their way.”

“Having morals is being a rebel now.”

“We were always rebels, you and I. Do you want to have a snack?”

“Sure. I was hoping to hang out with you before supper. I’ve got to get a start on my Philosophy essay later. It’s due tomorrow. That’s why I stayed so late at the library, doing research.”

“You never cease to amaze me. You wait till the night before to start all your essays. I don’t know how you do it. You manage to get a C+ every time, too.”

“I don’t set out to do it. I just forget about them until the day before.”

“It shows you’re really smart if you can write an essay in one night and get a C+. If anybody else tried to do what you do, they’d get an F or at least a D.”

“Thanks for the vote of confidence, Peg. I don’t think anybody else would describe me as smart.”

“But you are.”

“I had a lot of trouble in High School. It was much harder. University is fun and a lot easier. And a lot less hostile.”

"I've got some good news for you, sweetie." Peggy smiled mischievously, "Guess who's just moved back home?"

"Jack!" Dottie sprang up from her seat, "I knew he'd eventually leave that stuck-up bitch!"

"The aftermath is going to be a big mess. I don't even want to think about it."

"All that matters is she's out of his life, Peg." Dottie beamed, "The rest can take care of itself."

*   *   *

Outside Jack's door, she raised her hand in mid-air, unable to bring herself to knock. The door opened and Jack stood before her in the green striped shirt he knew she liked most. He was not wearing a tie. His arms pulled her into the office and enclosed her. His elbow nudged the door shut. He kissed her urgently, his tongue exploring every cavern of her mouth. Feeling his lips moving lower to her neck and sliding down to her cleavage, she moaned. His frenzied fingers tore her flimsy white gauze dress and pulled her lace camisole over her head, exposing her bare breasts.

She ripped his shirt open and caressed the downy blond hair on his chest. He pulled down her dress and half-slip to her knees as her fingers unbuckled his belt, unzipped his fly and slid his trousers to his ankles. Their bodies pressed close enough to dissolve into one another, they fell on the carpet, entangled and breathless. She longed to be crushed under his weight, to be devoured by his passion. His tongue circled her nipples. In one smooth sweep, he slid her silk panties down her legs. Arching her back, she grabbed at him urgently, drawing him to her. He wanted to be lost inside her and never return to reality. She was warm, fragrant, moist and welcoming. And she wanted him in a way no other woman had wanted him before. She was reaching out to the wounded child inside him, nurturing his fragile heart. She wanted him for who he was, as he was. She was surrendering not only her body, but her soul completely to him. He dissolved like hot wax on her chest, his head nestled between her breasts.

"I've never loved anyone the way I love you." he said.

"I never imagined anything this beautiful was even humanly possible." She lifted one hand to wipe her tears with her fingertips.

He kissed her breasts tenderly.

"There's no turning back now, Sydney."

Chapter 8/ Sparrows

The red brick Justice Building was set back from the street, behind an elaborate iron fence with a violet motif. Concrete steps led to four pink columns and three Gothic arches. Once inside the majestic edifice, one was struck by the incongruous interior. Sterile white walls, lowered ceilings and utilitarian industrial taupe carpeting over the original terrazzo, the antiseptic smell of recent renovations bore the stamp of the present decade. Every trace of character, originality, and craftsmanship from its Victorian heritage was obliterated.

It was exceptionally mild for a late Beavertown autumn. Rain was beating down on the pavement. Well-dressed crowds were scurrying to seek shelter, dark umbrellas bobbing rhythmically. The staccato of heels on the terrazzo entrance escalated to the beat of jungle drums in Sydney's chest. She stood against the side of the stairs, observing the steady stream of strangers arriving, shaking their umbrellas and parading past her, depositing droplets of rain on the sturdy carpet. Their footsteps became mercifully muted by the cushioned surface.

Willard Horncastle strode in, with his wilted gardenia of a wife, the ever-so-loyal Mildred. He was smug and stern in his pinstriped suit, proudly displaying his protruding abdomen and receding hairline. They were flanked by the dour Donald and the fickle Annette. Audrey strode in, tall, trim, upright, impeccably groomed and exceptionally attractive for her age. Dottie was straggling behind, tugging at her gabardine A-line skirt. With her fine dark hair pulled back in a small ponytail, she appeared more like a little girl than a university junior. She glanced uneasily in Sydney's direction, then averted her eyes and sped off after Audrey like a gazelle.

Diane and Gloria spotted Sydney from the entrance and approached her.

"How are you holding up?" Diane asked.

"All right, I guess."

"We'll be in there the whole time, rooting for you." Gloria said.

"I shall be watching Mr. Warren Horncastle very closely during these proceedings." Diane assured her, "When our paths cross in the future, I plan to be well-prepared. Remember everything we covered during the practice run? All the things you have to expect from his defense attorney?"

Sydney nodded.

"Don't worry. Everything's going to be all right. He cannot hurt you anymore, Sydney."

Voluptuous and pretty, with flawless black skin, Gloria listened in silence and placed a reassuring hand on Sydney's shoulder in parting as she and Diane headed to the courtroom.

Sydney caught her mother's smile at the far end of the corridor, entering through the side entrance, which had a wheelchair ramp, followed by her father being wheeled in by Ryan. Sydney ran to meet them and kissed both of them.

"How are you holding up, dear?" Edna stroked her hair, "Are you sure you're all right?"

"I'm just fine, Mom." she squeezed her hand.

Brett burst in through the front door, Marin at her arm, Maggie and Chuck following closely behind, Chuck guiding Maggie with each step. The sound of Maggie's cane landing tentatively on the three steps leading up to the lobby reverberated through the open space.

"Sweetheart!" Brett rushed to Sydney's side and enveloped her in a scented, lingering embrace. As Brett greeted Edna and Sid, Marin placed an arm around Sydney. Chuck shook her hand. The rotund, smiling Maggie, with her rhinestone-encrusted cat glasses and snow-white schoolgirl's blunt-cut hair, patted her back congenially.

Daisy and Greeney came up the stairs. Sydney ran to embrace Daisy, while Edna embraced Greeney.

"Thank you both for coming." Sydney said, turning to Greeney.

"If it weren't for this gracious lady here, I would have had a difficult time getting here." Daisy nodded toward Greeney.

"I go past your house on my way, Daisy." Greeney said.

Sydney positioned herself behind her father's wheelchair.

"Shall we go in?" he suggested.

The group proceeded toward the courtroom. Warren's cold dark eyes turned in her direction as she entered. He was impeccably groomed, every hair of his lionesque mane in place. With his perfectly chiseled features, deeply pronounced dimples, and expressively heavy eyebrows, he cast an impressive figure. His arrogant smirk followed her movements. She shrank into her seat, her eyes lowered, her shoulders stooped. His gaze was transfixed on her. On her left, Brett was fanning herself with a blank index card. Restless spectators in the aisles were exchanging pleasantries, the drone of their voices resembling a faulty air conditioner.

The doors facing them swung open, and Tony burst in, handsome in his navy trench coat. His knowing eyes met Brett's. Sydney glanced around her uneasily and caught sight of Jack in the back row, who discreetly waved at her.

The defense attorney regarded Diane with suspicion, and whispered in Warren's ear. Beth O'Brien was an athletic, muscular woman in her mid-thirties, dressed in an expensive mottled suit and sporting an excessive amount of glittering diamonds. Her serpent eyes combed the courtroom for scattered witnesses she intended to skewer. Sydney looked away from her.

Judge Clayton entered and the proceedings began. Diane had told her he was a fair judge – one of the best – and they were fortunate to have him assigned to the case. For the civil case,

Diane planned to push for a female judge, however, the province only had two of them.

"Your Honor, ladies and gentlemen of the jury, my colleague: Prosecution intends to show that Warren Horncastle is a callous, predatory man who raped Sydney Goldstein and Brett Morrow." Kitty Hawkins, the Crown Prosecutor, began her opening remarks, "This is a man who uses and discards women without a single thought. He is narcissistic and completely devoid of empathy or compassion. He objectifies women and exploits them to satisfy his own selfish desires. Prosecution intends to prove that is precisely what he did in this instance. Yes, Mr. Horncastle dated Miss Goldstein briefly. He soon became controlling and emotionally abusive, however, when she attempted to break free, he became indignant. He refused to take "no" for an answer. Warren Horncastle brutally raped Sydney Goldstein, causing her to have a miscarriage. Even when a woman said "no", he disregarded her wishes and took what he wanted. He was concerned only with his own gratification. Yes, he brutally raped her and left her bleeding. She begged him to get medical help for her, but he just walked away. He displayed wanton disregard for human life and suffering. He accused Miss Goldstein of becoming pregnant in order to convince him to marry her while she was pleading for help...Several months later, he executed a similar scenario when he raped Brett Morrow, to exact revenge from her – in his own words – because he blamed her for his breakup with Miss Goldstein. He believed Miss Morrow had somehow alienated Miss Goldstein from him. Warren Horncastle is a notorious womanizer who has sailed through life relying on his family's name and fortune, as well as his own good looks and superficial charm. He believes he is above the law...Please do not allow him to continue abusing women and making a mockery of our judicial system. He needs to be held accountable for his actions, just like everyone else. Warren Horncastle is guilty."

It was now Beth O'Brien's turn. Known as the most dynamic partner in "Horncastle, Horncastle and O'Brien", she boasted an impressive record: She never lost a case. She strutted up to the bench.

"Your Honor, ladies and gentlemen of the jury, my colleague: Warren Horncastle is an honest, hard-working man who has dedicated his life to helping shape young minds and creating productive citizens of the future. He has spent three decades contributing to this community and the future of our society." her arrogant smirk found Sydney and she fixed her eagle's gaze on her, slightly raising one of her eyebrows, "Then, in one fell swoop, it has been taken away from him. He has fallen victim to two delusional women claiming to have been sexually assaulted by him. Defense intends to show that these charges against him are nothing more than a plot by two bitter, vengeful women. Sydney Goldstein was a jilted lover, whose plans to trap Mr. Horncastle into marriage went awry. Brett Morrow was angry with him for exposing her sordid past to her prospective in-laws and preventing her from marrying Anthony Horncastle. The two women are friends. Together, they hatched a scheme to make Warren Horncastle pay for foiling their plans. Each one lured him to a deserted place to have sexual intercourse with him, and later claimed to be raped by him. Mr. Horncastle has been unduly humiliated. He has lost his teaching position. He has suffered enough. Please let justice be served and allow him to clear his good name."

Beth returned to her seat and whispered to Warren. Kitty began by calling peripheral witnesses to attest to Warren's roguish behavior and fast-paced lifestyle. His former colleagues from his teaching days cast him in a negative light. Female teachers from Beavertown High gave accounts of his inappropriate touching, lewd suggestions and his derogatory remarks about women in general. Upon cross-examination, they were reduced to tears by the burly Beth, who portrayed them as frustrated spinsters, ravenous for a man's attention and shamelessly infatuated with Warren. He had spurned their advances and now they were seeking revenge.

Dave Cagney, the brother of one of his countless former girlfriends, Marcia, was a more convincing witness. He recounted the verbal and psychological abuse heaped on his sister during the course of her relationship with Warren. The fact that Marcia was too distraught to come forward herself, however, did not bode favorably for the prosecution.

During the brief recess, to enable the prosecutor to meet with her upcoming witnesses, Marin led Brett outside. Sydney joined her parents. Edna held Sydney's hands in her own. Jack came up behind Sydney and stood awkwardly. Edna discreetly wheeled her husband away to allow them time alone.

"It's so hard to pretend we're only friends and colleagues." he whispered, "Until this is all over we can't afford to let anyone suspect the truth because it would hurt your case."

"Thank you for understanding."

"I love you."

"I love you, too."

The proceedings resumed. Kitty called a former Maitre' D from "The Castle", who had witnessed an altercation between Warren and a woman four or five years earlier.

He had noticed Warren become extremely agitated and throw a drink in the woman's face. Loud words had been exchanged. The woman had stormed out, never to be seen in the restaurant again.

Kitty called Sydney to the stand. Edna touched her shoulder and whispered.

"You'll be just fine, darling."

Sydney rose and turned around to exchange quick, furtive glances with Jack. On the witness stand, she stated her name and swore on the Bible. In accordance with Kitty's questions, she recounted the events of the evening Warren had violated her. She astonished even herself with her composure. She had earlier refused the offer of pharmaceutical help from her doctor.

"Thank you, Miss Goldstein." Kitty smiled congenially; in her classic forest green suit, she was dignified and slender. Her traditional pageboy haircut and horn-rimmed glasses lent her an air of approachability and no-nonsense dependability. She appeared, however, less like the sharp-witted prosecutor who had put away an impressive number of criminals and more like a kind neighbor.

Sydney searched the stern faces of the jury. Most appeared to be middle-aged and middle class: Civil servants, perhaps. Some might be mothers. No mother could condone Warren's treatment of women. And, no mother could feel fondness for the meaty barracuda who was baring her fangs before Sydney now. Beth O'Brien's imposing figure sent a chill throughout the courtroom. In the back row, Diane was glaring at Beth with those intense cerulean pools, cutting through her false veneer like a straight-edged razor.

"Your name was not always Goldstein, was it? Were you not using a different name when you first arrived in Beavertown?"

"Yes."

"What name were you going by, then?"

"Bertrand."

"Why is that, Miss Goldstein?"

"It was my married name."

"Are you still married, then?"

"No. I'm divorced."

"What year were you divorced?"

"1961."

"What province were you married in, Miss Goldstein?"

"Quebec."

"In that province, women are not required to take their husbands' names. Were you aware of this when you got married?"

"Yes."

"And you chose not to maintain your maiden name. Did you have a reason for this?"

"Yes. I was not raised by my real parents. My stepfather abducted me when I was very young. He and his common-law wife did not treat me well and I did not wish to hang on to their name."

"What did you do following your divorce? How did you support yourself?"

"I waited on tables, did cleaning work, and eventually sang in clubs."

"For the entire time until you came here? The entire fifteen years?"

"Yes."

"Is that the only thing you did to support yourself?"

"Yes."

"It couldn't have paid too well."

"No, but I didn't mind."

"Did you supplement your meagre income with other things on the side?"

"No." she said firmly.

"Montreal is a big city, Miss Goldstein. Most clubs have strippers and prostitutes. These clubs are frequently owned by members of organized crime. Are you insulting our intelligence by expecting us to believe that an attractive woman in financial need would turn down the opportunity to raise her standard of living?"

"Yes. Because it is true."

"I am sure it is, Miss Goldstein. The Tooth Fairy and the Easter Bunny are also real."

Self-conscious snickers swept over the courtroom.

"During those fifteen years in Montreal, did you date much?"

"No."

"Why is that?"

"I didn't meet the kind of men I wanted to date."

"And what kind is that? Wealthy?"

"No. Nice."

"Now, then, Miss Goldstein, let's just fast forward to three and a half years ago, when you first arrived in Beavertown. What was your reason for moving?"

"I had learned my biological parents were here."

"Shortly after your arrival, you met the defendant, Warren Horncastle, did you not?"

"Yes."

"He asked you to go out on a date with him and you accepted. Is that right?"

"Yes."

"Miss Goldstein, is it not true that you went to bed with him on your first date?"

"Yes." she murmured, biting her lower lip.

"Please speak up, Miss Goldstein."

"Yes."

"And you continued dating Mr. Horncastle for several months, did you not?"

"Yes."

"You maintained a sexual relationship with him?"

"Yes."

"Were you dating other men during this time?"

"No."

"So, Warren Horncastle was your only sexual partner?"

"Yes."

"What was the reason you wanted to be with Mr. Horncastle? Was it the fact that he was "nice", as you put it?"

"No. I was physically attracted to him."

"Miss Goldstein, were you, in fact, pregnant at the time of the alleged assault?"

"Yes."

"How far along were you?"

"Three months."

"You claimed it was not Mr. Horncastle's child. Yet you've just told us you had a monogamous relationship."

"We did not have a monogamous relationship. During the time we were dating, Warren was seeing other women. He made it clear at the outset he was not interested in a monogamous relationship. In fact, by midsummer, we were no longer dating regularly or having sexual relations."

"You must have been pretty upset about that. Is that why you decided to get pregnant as a last ditch attempt to get Mr. Horncastle to commit?"

"No. My pregnancy was not planned."

"All the same, you must have seen it as an opportunity to get him to marry you."

"The baby was not Warren's."

"You've told us you were not seeing any other men."

"I was not. I had also stopped seeing Warren before I became pregnant. There was no possible way for it to be Warren's."

"Then, whose was it?"

"Someone I met in Toronto." she murmured.

"Speak up, Miss Goldstein."

"Someone I met in Toronto."

"Where did you meet him?"

"At a bar."

"And, are you in the habit of picking up men in bars?"

"No. That was the only time."

"Did you contact this man to inform him that he was about to become a father?"

"No."

"Why not?"

"I didn't know how to contact him."

"Come, come, Miss Goldstein, isn't it a fact that the child you were carrying was Mr. Horncastle's?"

"No!"

"Isn't it also a fact that you dated Warren Horncastle for the prestige of being seen with a member of the Beavertown elite? You dreamed of a life of luxury as only the Horncastles could enjoy, to make up for the years of poverty and deprivation you suffered in Montreal? When you realized he had no intentions of marrying you, you decided to strike back in revenge."

"That is not true."

"Have you been involved in other relationships since you and Mr. Horncastle parted?"

"No."

"You have not picked up other men in bars as you did in Toronto?"

"No."

"Miss Goldstein, have you sworn to celibacy for the rest of your life?"

"Objection, Your Honor!" Kitty sprang to her feet, "Miss Goldstein's sex life is irrelevant!"

"On the contrary," Beth said, "The way she relates to men is very relevant."

"I'll grant you leniency, Mrs. O'Brien, but you must show relevance." The judge said.

Edna wondered about Sydney's lost child. Her Sydney would not engage in casual sex. The baby's father had to have been someone she knew. Someone she cared about and trusted. She was protecting someone. But who? Was it another Horncastle? Someone at work?

"Miss Goldstein, you must have had numerous opportunities on your job at Chandler's Lounge where you are presently employed, to meet men. Yet you are saying that you have not been on a date for two years. Why is that?"

"The patrons of Chandler's are mainly married couples. It's not a place where singles meet."

"Or perhaps you just can't seem to get men interested in you."

"Objection, Your Honor! "

"Mrs. O'Brien, keep your speculation to yourself."

"Yes, Your Honor." Beth scowled, "Do you think that your "touch-me-not "attitude keeps men away? You might be sending subconscious messages."

"I don't think so. I may not be outgoing, but I certainly don't do anything to put men off."

"Isn't it true Miss Goldstein, that you really don't like men at all?"

"That is not true."

"Isn't it true, Miss Goldstein, that your sexual preference leans toward women? Aren't you, in fact, in love with your colleague and friend, Brett Morrow?"

"Objection, Your Honor!" Kitty cried indignantly, "My colleague is out of line!"

"No more questions, Your Honor." Beth smirked.

"You may step down, Miss Goldstein." the judge said, "This court will adjourn until 2 p.m."

Sydney bolted out of the courtroom without a word or a glance.

* * *

They resumed their seats in the still half-empty courtroom. Sydney spotted a familiar face by the door: A plain woman with limp dark brown hair and dark-rimmed glasses. She remembered her from the club: She had been Tony's date. What was her name? Leona? No. It was more unusual. Leah – that was it. Only, she spelled it without an "h". It was a name one did not hear anymore. After much hesitation, Lea selected a seat in the back row. Sydney hoped Brett would not see her. The doors behind them swung open to allow a herd of spectators into the courtroom. Among them was Celia. Her heart sank. Had she been there in the morning during her testimony? No doubt, she had been gloating. The next time they met, she would likely have plenty of disparaging remarks to make about her.

Kitty's first witness for the afternoon was Chuck. As he walked past Brett in his teal suit, he flashed a peace sign at her.

"Please state your name."

"Charles Cedric Seabrook III."

The name was recognized by everyone as belonging to the son of a sea captain from St. Bartholomew, the coastal village where New Brunswick aristocracy resided.

"Mr. Seabrook, please tell the court the events of the early hours of July 11, 1977."

"I was asleep. Then, around three o'clock, my phone rang. It was Sydney. She sounded pretty upset. She said that someone had done something dreadful to Brett, and they needed me to drive them to the hospital. I jumped out of bed immediately and drove to the club."

"And, what did you see when you got there, Mr. Seabrook?"

"Brett was messed up pretty bad. Her face was bleeding, her lip cut and swollen. She was curled up in a corner, trembling. She didn't even seem to notice when I came in."

"What transpired next?"

"Sydney helped me gather her up and carry her out to the car. I placed her across the back seat. Sydney sat beside her and held her the entire time."

"And, did either Miss Morrow or Miss Goldstein say who had done this to Miss Morrow?"

"No. I don't think even Sydney knew at that time."

"Mr. Seabrook, how long have you known Miss Morrow?"

"Six – no, seven years."

"How would you describe the nature of your relationship?"

"Very dear friends." he glanced affectionately at Brett, who smiled at him, "Brett is a beautiful person."

"Would you say you were ever romantically involved?"

"No. Just very good friends."

"Mr. Seabrook, what do you do for a living?"

"I'm a musician. I play piano at Chandler's Lounge, and accompany all the singers."

"You and Miss Morrow are co-workers, then. Is that how you met?"

"Yes. Both of us have been at Chandler's since it first opened."

Kitty continued questioning Chuck, and concluded by thanking him. Beth strode up to the box, smirking deliciously.

"Mr. Seabrook," she turned to look at Brett, "You have known Miss Morrow for seven years, and you say that you were only friends. Does that mean your relationship is completely platonic?"

"That is right."

"Brett Morrow is undeniably an exceptionally beautiful woman. Have you ever secretly wished you could have a sexual relationship with her?"

"No. Brett is a very dear friend and I love her very much, but it has never been sexual with us. Yes, she's exceptionally beautiful. I am aware of that. I would have to be blind not to."

"Mr. Seabrook, is it not true that the reason you are not physically attracted to Miss Morrow is, you're a homosexual?"

"Your Honor, irrelevant!" Kitty protested.

"I plan to show relevance, Your Honor."

"I'll allow it, but you're on thin ice, Mrs. O'Brien."

"Thank you. Please answer the question, Mr. Seabrook."

"Yes."

"And, were you not a victim of gay bashing some years ago?"

"Yes."

"You were seriously injured during the attack?"

"Yes."

"And, Miss Morrow was very supportive of you during your ordeal, was she not?"

"Yes, she was."

"You owe her a great deal, don't you, Mr. Seabrook?"

"We're friends. We don't keep score."

"But you would do anything for her, would you not?"

"We are friends. I would try to provide as much support for her as I could."

"You would stand behind her."

"Yes."

"And would that include lying for her?"

"Objection!" Kitty intercepted.

"No more questions, Your Honor." Beth said smugly.

"Mrs. Hawkins, your next witness."

"Prosecution calls Miss Brett Morrow."

Sydney squeezed Brett's hand as she rose. In her dark suit, Brett appeared vulnerable and frail.

Kitty took her back to the earlier part of the evening she was assaulted, up to the time Jack was called away by Linda and he requested that Brett lock up.

"Miss Morrow, please tell the court what took place later on that night, rather, early morning."

"I was getting ready to lock up. I heard someone behind me in the corridor. I thought it might be Jack coming back. I called out to him, but there was no answer. Then, Warren – Mr. Horncastle – came right up bchind me."

"Were you afraid?"

"I was startled. But not afraid. I did not have reason to believe Warren might be a threat."

"Did he state his business?"

"Yes. Initially, I thought he was looking for Sydney, and I told him she wasn't there. He said he was there to see me."

"Did he seem intoxicated?"

"Not particularly."

"Was he angry?"

"He seemed agitated."

"What did you tell him?"

"I was extremely tired and I told him so. I told him I didn't have the energy to exchange barbs with him."

"Was that a customary thing, exchanging barbs?"

"Yes. Every time Warren and I ran into each other, we made sarcastic comments about one another."

"Is this what you believed he had in mind on that occasion?"

"Yes."

"Did he persist when you stated you were tired?"

"Yes. He seemed particularly determined. Possessed, almost."

"Objection! Speculation!" Beth cried out.

"Overruled."

"Did Mr. Horncastle tell you he was particularly upset and if so, why, Miss Morrow?" Kitty continued.

"Yes. He was upset about the break-up of his relationship with Sydney and he blamed me for it."

"Blamed you? How?"

"Warren believed I had somehow influenced Sydney in some way and turned her against him."

"And, had you?"

"Of course not. Sydney has her own mind. I made no secret of the fact that I had my qualms about their involvement, but it had no impact on the way things transpired. What drove Sydney away was Warren's own behavior, not anything I said. He refused to see that."

"What did he say to you?"

"He said: 'You're going to get what you deserve, bitch!'."

"What happened after that, Miss Morrow?"

"He took me back to the dressing room and threw me on the floor. He was in a rage. He..." she dabbed at her eyes with a tissue.

"Take your time, Miss Morrow. Take a few minutes to compose yourself."

Brett lifted her chin and faced her attacker in the eye as she recounted the way he had violated her.

"Thank you, Miss Morrow." Kitty smiled, "Your witness, Mrs. O'Brien."

"Miss Morrow," Beth stood menacingly before her, "How long have you known Mr. Warren Horncastle?"

"Approximately seven years."

"How well did you know him? Did you socialize frequently with him?"

"No. We did not socialize. I ran into him occasionally at The Castle. I knew him as Tony's uncle."

"What was the nature of your relationship?"

"Acquaintances, I would say."

"You were only acquaintances, yet you felt entitled to make moral judgments against him?"

"I was not judging him. His reputation was well-known."

"Did Mr. Horncastle ever extend an invitation to you? Suggest anything of a romantic nature?"

"No."

"So, you saw him night after night, with a different woman on his arm, enjoying himself, and yet despite his keen eye for beautiful women, he never once asked you out on a date?"

"Yes, that is right."

"Did that make you feel resentful, Miss Morrow? Was it a blow to your ego that he did not find you attractive?"

"No. We were not each other's type."

"Did you not feel slighted in the least that he did not pay any attention to you as a woman?"

"No."

"In fact, Miss Morrow, were you not jealous when Mr. Horncastle displayed more than a passing interest in your friend, Miss Goldstein? Isn't that the real reason you wanted to break them up?"

"No. The reason I did not approve was that I was worried he would hurt Sydney. I knew he wasn't capable of making a commitment."

"It was your altruistic desire to spare your friend from heartbreak that was behind your antagonistic remarks, then. Is that right?"

"I didn't want him to mess with her head."

"That was very noble of you, Miss Morrow. Even before Miss Goldstein entered the picture, were you not always needling Mr. Horncastle, never missing an opportunity to put him down a notch or two?"

"It was all in fun. Exchanging barbs was our way of relating to one another."

"Or was it simply a way to mask sexual tension?"

"Absolutely not."

"Miss Morrow, who was it that first introduced you to Warren Horncastle?"

"It was Anthony Horncastle, his nephew."

"What was your relationship with Anthony Horncastle?"

"We dated."

"Just dated? Wasn't it much more than that, Miss Morrow? Were you two not planning marriage?"

"Yes."

"And, how did Warren Horncastle react to his nephew taking up with an older woman who had a colorful past?"

"He wasn't very happy about it."

"How did the rest of the family feel?"

"The same as Warren."

"In fact, Warren Horncastle was instrumental in turning the rest of his family against you, was he not?"

"I suppose so."

"What happened to your relationship with Anthony Horncastle as a result of his family's disapproval?"

"We broke off our engagement."

"Who initiated the break-up? You or him?"

"I did. I didn't want to cause a rift between Tony and his family."

"Or, perhaps, you knew his family was threatening to disown him if he married you."

"I didn't want Tony to suffer as a result of our relationship."

"So, you ended the engagement, but continued seeing him on the sly and reaping the benefits of his family's affluence?"

"No. We were in love. We couldn't just walk away from each other."

"Yet you felt Miss Goldstein could walk away from Warren Horncastle easily if you kept reminding her of his shortcomings."

"I was worried Sydney was getting in over her head."

"Miss Morrow, did you not have a grudge against the entire Horncastle family for coming between you and the man you loved?"

"No."

"Miss Morrow, did you and Anthony Horncastle maintain a monogamous relationship after your engagement was officially called off?"

"Not exactly."

"In fact, you flaunted other men in his face, did you not?"

"No. It wasn't like that."

"You have a weakness for younger men – the younger the better; isn't that a fact, Miss Morrow?"

"No."

"In fact, was it not your voracious sexual appetite that led to the demise of both of your marriages?"

"No. My first marriage ended following the loss of our daughter. My second marriage ended for totally different reasons."

"How many children do you have, Miss Morrow?"

"Four."

"Is it not true that you have been estranged from your daughter Laurel Samson for several years?"

"Laurie and I have had our problems. All parents have rough periods with their children."

"You are not even aware that your daughter Laurel has married a rock musician named Rusty Nail in Los Angeles, are you?"

The look of utter astonishment that swept across Brett's face was all Beth needed for the effect she desired. Brett's eyes sought out Josh's. Sydney strained her neck to spot him in the back row. The vacant expression in his eyes told her that, he, too, had not known about it before this.

"What was the reason for your estrangement from your daughter, Miss Morrow?"

"Divorce is difficult on children."

"Particularly if their mother goes out to bars and brings home an assortment of men on a regular basis."

"Your Honor, I object!" Kitty protested, "Inflammatory."

"Sustained. I don't want to keep warning you, Mrs. O'Brien."

"Yes, Your Honor. Miss Morrow, your daughter had to assume the role of the parent for her two younger brothers and for her own mother, did she not?"

"Those were very trying times for all of us."

"As soon as she was old enough, your daughter went to a private school in Connecticut, near one of your sisters, did she not?"

"She decided that would be best for her."

"Laurel has completely disowned you, has she not?"

"Mothers and daughters can have difficult times."

"How do you get along with your other children?"

"We're all very close." she smiled, making eye contact with Marin.

"Your sons were much too young to understand what was happening during that time, were they not? Laurel shielded them from the pain."

"I realize I did not exercise good judgment at that time, and I have spent each day since then repenting the error of my ways."

"I understand you have another daughter: The daughter from your first marriage, who was accidentally switched at the hospital and raised by another couple. The child of yours who died was actually theirs. You have been reunited with your biological daughter. How is your relationship?"

"It's wonderful." she smiled, gazing at Marin, "She is my guiding star."

"Miss Morrow, you say you regret the choices you made following your divorce, however, you have done little in the way of making an atonement for your past wrongdoings. You sing at a bar and continue to pursue a sordidly active sex life. You have made no attempts to modify your lifestyle."

"That is not true."

"The court heard earlier about your close friendship with Mr. Seabrook. Do you have other male friends who are homosexual?"

"Some."

"And you permit these men to be near your growing sons?"

"Gay men are not a threat to young boys. They like grown men. The majority of pedophiles are heterosexual men."

"Thank you for the Psychology lesson, Miss Morrow. Do you have lesbian friends, as well?"

"Some."

"Is it not true, Miss Morrow, that you enjoy a bisexual lifestyle?"

"Your Honor, my colleague's badgering the witness!" Kitty sprang to her feet.

"Mrs. O'Brien, change your line of questioning."

"Your Honor, I plan to show relevance."

"Then, get to it, Mrs. O'Brien. We're all growing old waiting for you to show relevance."

"Yes, Your Honor. Miss Morrow, were you not resentful of Warren Horncastle because you wished to form a sexual union with Miss Goldstein yourself?"

"Sydney and I are the dearest of friends. We are not and never have been lovers."

"You say you are good friends. You confide in each other, then, do you not, as all friends do?"

"Of course we do."

"Then, Miss Goldstein must have disclosed the identity of her baby's father to you."

"All I know is what she has told the court."

"Come, come, Miss Morrow, do you expect the court to believe that?"

"Yes I do, because it is true."

"Miss Morrow, you are under oath."

"I realize that, and I'm telling you that is all I know."

"It was Warren Horncastle, was it not? Did she not have a plan to trap him into marriage, so she could enjoy the type of lifestyle the Horncastle name provides? A penniless woman from the slums of Montreal, scratching out a living for decades by singing in sleazy, smoky bars...Was it not her dream to marry into money and live a life of leisure?"

"No. She's not poor anymore. Her biological parents are the Goldsteins."

"The Goldsteins are nowhere near as affluent as the Horncastles, though, are they? The Horncastles are the elite, the aristocracy of this region."

"Sydney had not been intimate with Warren for much too long for the baby to be his."

"Perhaps she was further along in her pregnancy than she claimed to be."

"Objection, Your Honor! Speculation!"

"Sustained. Mrs. O'Brien, change your line of questioning."

"Yes, Your Honor. Miss Morrow, do you not have a drinking problem? Didn't your drinking contribute to the rift between yourself and your daughter Laurel?"

"I do drink sometimes. But I don't have a problem."

"Wouldn't you agree that alcohol has been a contributing factor in your poor judgment?"

"Occasionally, I might have one too many."

"But it is not occasionally. You drink heavily on a regular basis, don't you, Miss Morrow?"

"Not heavily."

"Was it not your drinking problem that led to the break-up of both your marriages?"

"My first marriage broke up when the child we raised as our daughter died of a congenital heart defect. The strain was more than both of us could handle."

"As a result of that tragedy, you began relying more and more on the bottle, did you not?"

"I had lost my baby. Losing a child is not a minor loss. I would like to see how you would handle it – if you actually had a heart."

"Miss Morrow, you are dangerously close to being cited for contempt." the judge said.

Quivering, Brett lowered her eyes.

"No more questions, Your Honor."

Sydney led her outside to safety, and temporary anonymity. In the crisp air, she walked beside her, to the sanctuary of the Goldstein bungalow.

Chapter 9/ Deaf Hearts

Shielded from view by the two portly men in front of her, she peered through the glass doors in the vestry. In the rose-colored arched enclosure, the two of them were engaged in an animated exchange: She, fashionably thin and elongated by black stilettos, tossing her waist-length brown hair suggestively, stealing furtive glances at men walking past on the street. And, he, silent and still, shrinking with her each word.

"They don't seem to be getting along, do they?" she heard a voice behind her.

"Celia. Hello."

"Don't get your hopes up, dear. It'll soon blow over and they'll be tearing each other's clothes off."

"I don't know what you mean."

"You're chasing an impossible dream, Sydney."

Sydney peered directly into Celia's small eyes. Her height gave her an advantage at moments like this.

"I'm sure I don't know what you mean."

"Hmm…It's obvious to the entire world that you are hopelessly in love with him." the wiry woman tucked her dull brown hair behind her ears, "You're wasting your time, dear. He'll never want you. Don't make a fool of yourself. I think he's a good friend to you, am I right? Just count your blessings. He does care. Just not the way you wish. Can you understand that? Men like Jack don't fall for women like you, dear. Don't waste your time and energy pining away for him. He's an international recording star. He gets invited to Hollywood parties. He meets glamorous women."

The couple outside still seemed to be engaged in their quarrel. The female flung a cigarette in his direction and flapped her arms like a hungry pigeon. She stamped her foot and stormed off. Sydney longed to run to him, however, Celia's presence crippled her. He struck up a conversation outside with an elderly man. Celia smirked, enjoying Sydney's discomfort.

"You really ought to get some professional help for your relationship issues, dear." Celia said, "I can fit you in next Tuesday, but I must warn you, my fees are high. If you miss an appointment, you still have to pay, unless you cancel twenty-four hours ahead of time."

"No thanks. I'm fine."

"You are not fine. I wish you had come to me for help before you got yourself into this whole mess."

"There is no mess."

"Come on. This whole farce – accusing your old boyfriend of rape. You were frustrating him with your sexual inadequacies and hang-ups. What would you expect any normal man to do? I'm not surprised he left you. Your emotional immaturity, your clinginess would drive anyone anyway. You are so needy."

"You don't even know what you're talking about, Celia. And, if you think I'm such a terrible person, why are you standing around wasting your time talking to me?"

"Obviously, I've hit a nerve. And, I'm only here because I'm meeting a friend. You don't have to stand around, you know. You can go in and take your seat."

"I'm waiting for a friend myself."

"I don't think Brett would be too disappointed if you weren't here. She's being kind and gracious, dear, but it's obvious she means more to you than you do to her. You're suffocating her with your neediness. She feels so indebted to you for your support, she doesn't have the heart to pull away from this unhealthy relationship."

"She would have told me if she felt that way."

"She's too tender-hearted to hurt your feelings. She would never tell you that you are too clingy and dependent, or that you're smothering her."

"Why don't you try minding your own business for a change and leave me alone?"

"Tut, tut. Be careful. Your roots are showing. Mongrels don't speak to colonels' wives that way. Especially mongrels of mixed ethnicity, undetermined sexuality, women bearing men's names."

Sydney stood by the glass doors and kept her back to her, choosing not to dignify her last remark with a response. She kept her gaze outward. Jack was still with the elderly man. Brett rounded the corner, running like a deer with the agility of a teenaged sprinter. She came bounding up the stairs in her pink wool suit, her curls falling loose from her up-do and swaying behind her.

"I'm sorry, sweetheart!" she pushed the door open and ran to embrace Sydney, "The line at the bank was so long! I had to go at lunch, because they close so early, we'd never be out of here in time. We could be tied up in here until all hours."

"You're right."

"Shall we go in, sweetheart?" she glanced quizzically at Celia as she led her away, "Are you okay, sweetheart? Was that woman bothering you?"

"Celia's a busybody. She's getting too big for her breeches because she's working on her M.Ed. and people are actually paying some attention to her."

"That's my girl. You're learning to place blame where it belongs and not internalizing it."

The courtroom appeared less crowded, perhaps because it was the first sunny day since the beginning of the trial. Bands of sunlight crept in through the slats of the sterile white Venetian blinds and rested on the sisal carpet.

Beth's early witnesses were liquor store clerks and bartenders from less than respectable establishments. Walking with the aid of canes and crutches, some had to have been hauled out of deep retirement to testify. The general consensus was that Brett guzzled booze like nobody's business and flirted with every man within close proximity. Three of Warren's former girlfriends were also called upon to testify that he had treated them well and he was the sort of man they realized had to be accepted as he was: You enjoyed the finer things in life with him, had some laughs, then, moved on. He was not the marrying kind, or even the kind to be tied down to a serious relationship. The idea of him committing sexual assault was absolutely ludicrous, they emphasized; he had a bevy of nubile women all willing and eager to give themselves to him.

During the recess, Marin engaged Brett in a hushed conversation. Edna and Sid leaned forward to encourage Sydney as she and Jack exchanged tender glances. Court was called to order. Young Andy was called upon to testify. He tripped on his way to the witness box, cursed under his breath, and shook his shaggy blond mane out of his eyes. Seated on the edge of his seat, he tapped one foot and spoke in a barely audible murmur as he recounted in gory detail the humiliating evening Brett had seduced him.

"What did Miss Morrow do when you returned with her prescription, Mr. Darling?"

"Um...She told me to go into her dressing room."

"What was she doing?"

"Sitting at the table."

"And how was she dressed?"

"Um...in a sort of see-through thing."

"What did she say to you? Mr. Darling, please tell the court what transpired after you went into Miss Morrow's dressing room."

"She...um...sort of started saying stuff like...um, did I think she was pretty...um, how old I was, and stuff...She wasn't, like, wearing too much."

"Were you frightened by such aggressive advances, Mr. Darling?"

"Your Honor, my colleague's leading the witness!"

"Sustained."

"How did you feel?" Beth rephrased her question.

"I dunno." Andy shrugged, "Okay, I guess."

"And, did Miss Morrow ultimately lure you into a tryst that evening?"

"Duh – I don't know what that means."

"Did Miss Morrow lure you to have sexual intercourse with her?"

"Yeah." he beamed.

Brett pulled her shoulders forward and lowered her head. Sydney massaged her shoulder and stroked her cheek. She produced a roll of Tropical Lifesavers from her pocketbook and offered one to Brett. She took a green one and popped it into her mouth. Sydney dabbed at Brett's eyes with a blue tissue she also fished out of her pocketbook.

Kitty was up front, cross-examining Andy.

"Mr. Darling, did you witness your male colleagues talking about Miss Morrow on sexual terms?"

"I dunno."

"Please answer yes or no, Mr. Darling."

"Um, yes."

"What was the content of these conversations?"

"I dunno. They said she was a fox. A babe."

"And, translated into regular language, that means?"

"She was nice-looking."

"Was there further talk about her attributes, and how they felt about them?"

"Um...They said her tits...her breasts...were hanging out all the time."

"On the stage?"

"Yes."

"What was Miss Morrow's attire when she was singing?"

"Dresses." he appeared puzzled.

"Formal or casual?"

"Formal."

"Have other female performers at Chandler's dressed similarly?"

"Yes."

"Were their breasts also "hanging out", as you put it?"

"Yes."

"Did your colleagues remark on them, as well?"

"Sometimes. Not as much."

"Why is that?"

"Brett...she...flirted a lot."

"Did she make suggestive remarks? Did she attempt to get to know any of them better?"

"Um, no. She was...playful...real friendly."

"Is Miss Morrow friendly with other people, as well? Women, children, senior citizens?"

"Yes."

"Would you say she's a friendly, approachable person?"

"Yes."

"On the night in question, when you had sexual relations with her, did she appear the same as usual?"

"Um...dunno."

"When Miss Morrow arrived at work, did she seem happy?"

"Um...not really."

"Did she appear different in any way?"

"Yeah...She was kinda quiet. Like she was cryin' or somethin'."

"Did she tell you what was on her mind?"

"Nope."

"So, you were aware she did not appear her usual self."

"Yeah."

"That, in fact, was the day her daughter Laurel had walked out on her. Were you ever informed of that, Mr. Darling?"

"Yeah. Johnny mentioned it a coupla days later."

"Thank you, Mr. Darling. No more questions."

"Call your next witness, Mrs. O'Brien." the judge said.

"Defense calls Dr. Joshua Samson, Your Honor. If it pleases the court, Defense would like it known that Dr. Samson is a hostile witness."

"It's noted."

"Dr. Samson, please state your relationship to Miss Morrow." Beth ordered as he was barely sworn in.

"She is my ex-wife." his eyes met Brett's and lingered.

"What is your present relationship like with each other?"

"We are on good terms."

"Do you see each other frequently?"

"We share custody of our two sons."

"How would you describe her parenting skills?"

"Brett's a wonderful mother. She's loving, supportive and selfless. She puts the boys first."

"She was not always a model parent, though, was she, Dr. Samson?"

"I don't know what you mean. Brett's always been a great mom."

"Isn't it true, Dr. Samson, that, after the two of you divorced, Miss Morrow led a life of reckless abandon? Did she not leave the children unattended while she caroused around town with men?"

"I am not aware of any such thing."

"Dr. Samson, is it not true Social Services were contacted by neighbors?"

"I am not aware of that."

"Dr. Samson, Social Services contacted you, did they not?"

"I...can't remember."

"Dr. Samson, you are under oath. Please answer the question."

"I can't remember. It was a long time ago."

"Dr. Samson, you are dangerously close to being in contempt of court." the judge said, "Answer the question."

"They might have called me, yes. But the allegations were unfounded. It was a malicious neighbor with too much time on her hands."

"Dr. Samson, did your wife have a drinking problem?"

"No."

"Did she not drink several martinis each day?"

"So do a lot of people."

"Is your wife an alcoholic?"

"Your Honor, I object to this line of questioning!" Kitty said, "Counsel is clearly badgering the witness!"

"Sustained."

"No more questions, Your Honor." Beth smirked.

Kitty took her place in front of him. Josh leaned back.

"Dr. Samson, you mentioned your wife lost her child – or the child she had raised as her own, as it was revealed during earlier testimonies. She faced another stressful event in her life shortly following that loss, did she not?"

"Yes. Her marriage broke up and she faced life on her own."

"And she survived, apparently. When you met her, how was she coping?"

"She was a vibrant, exuberant woman."

"Was your marriage happy?"

"Very happy."

"You had three children together, am I right?"

"Yes."

"And, was she a good, responsible mother to them?"

"Yes. The very best."

"Would you say she behaved like a rational, stable person?"

"Objection! The witness is not an expert in Psychology!" Beth bellowed.

"I am only asking for a personal opinion, not an expert one, Your Honor."

"I'll allow it."

"She's the most stable person I know."

"Would you say she has displayed the ability to cope reasonably well with the tragedies life has thrown at her?"

"Brett's coped remarkably well. I don't see how anyone could have done better. They would have to be totally devoid of feeling."

"Thank you, Dr. Samson. That will be all."

Josh cast a pained glance at Brett on his way back to his seat.

"Mrs. O'Brien, call your next witness."

"Your Honor, Defense calls Anthony Horncastle. Mr. Horncastle is also a hostile witness."

"Duly noted."

Erect and trim in a custom-tailored navy suit, he betrayed no emotion as he was sworn in.

"Mr. Horncastle, please tell the court what you do for a living."

"I'm an attorney."

"Are you a partner with your family's law firm?"

"No. I'm in private practice."

"Were you, in fact, at one time working at the family firm?"

"Yes."

"What was your reason for leaving?"

"I wanted to work independently."

"Did you not get into disputes with your father and uncle on a regular basis?"

"We might not have seen eye to eye at times. That's inevitable."

"Were you, in fact, not fired from your position at your family's law firm, Mr. Horncastle?"

"Objection! Relevance!"

"Sustained."

"I plan to show relevance."

"Then, get to it, Counsel."

"Were you not, in fact, fired because of your family's disapproval of Miss Morrow? Didn't your family also threaten to disown you?"

"Yes."

"That must have made you feel resentful."

"I got over it."

"Your engagement to Miss Morrow was broken, was it not, shortly following their ultimatum?"

"Yes."

"Then you were affected by their ultimatum, if you broke your engagement."

"I was not the one who broke it." he said softly.

"Why do you suppose Miss Morrow broke it off?"

"She did not wish to come between my family and myself. She did not wish to be the cause of family strife."

"So, her motives were altruistic?"

"Yes."

"Or, perhaps, she was only interested in marrying you for the money you'd be inheriting and the extravagant lifestyle you'd be providing for her?"

"No." he asserted forcefully.

"Mr. Horncastle, who was largely instrumental in convincing your family Miss Morrow was an inappropriate choice of a partner for you?"

"My uncle, Warren Horncastle."

"And, how did he accomplish it?"

"He embellished things he had heard about her."

"Did he not, in fact, witness firsthand the way Miss Morrow conducted herself in public?"

"That was his claim."

"Miss Morrow was aware of your uncle's role in your family's reaction to her, was she not?"

"Yes."

"Did she not feel antagonistic toward him?"

"I suppose."

"What about you, Mr. Horncastle? Were you not angry with your uncle?"

"Yes."

"Did you wish to exact revenge?"

"No. Why would I?"

"What about Miss Morrow?"

"Of course not."

"Was she not heard publicly threatening him?"

"I don't know of any such thing!" he laughed nervously.

"Really? Was she not overheard at Chandler's, saying:" she glanced swiftly at a cue card in her hand, "'Some day, Warren, you'll get yours!'?"

"I don't recall. They were always kidding around."

"After Miss Morrow broke off your engagement, did the two of you stop seeing each other?"

"No. We work closely at Chandler's. I fill in when my cousin and business partner Jack Chandler's away on tour."

"Over the course of three or four years since your break-up, have you and Miss Morrow had a platonic relationship? Purely a business relationship?"

"We have remained friends."

"Define 'friends', Mr. Horncastle. Is it friends as in going to a hockey game together?" she said sarcastically, "Or does it involve other benefits? Have you not, in fact, maintained an on-again-off-again intimate relationship discreetly all this time?"

"That is irrelevant." he scoffed.

"It is relevant."

"I don't see how." he stated in a confrontational manner, acquired through years of practice on the other side of the witness box.

"You must answer the question Mr. Horncastle."

"Yes." he said grudgingly.

"So, Miss Morrow has remained your lover, waiting in the sidelines for you to inherit your fortune, so the two of you can live the life of opulence she's always dreamed of, once the obstacles are removed."

"That's preposterous! You're making us out to be mercenaries." he retorted in a measured voice.

"No more questions." Beth strutted back to her seat.

Edna searched Tony's face. She had known him since his days as a brash young attorney in the family firm. Now, he was a distinguished, quietly confident man, trim and handsome, greying at the temples with that air of distinction. Even through Beth's fire breathing, he had retained his composure.

Kitty strode up with a compassionate gleam in her eye.

"Mr. Horncastle, approximately a year following the initial break-up of your engagement to Miss Morrow, both of you dated others, did you not?"

"That is right."

"Was Miss Morrow dating David Carlson of John's Bay, the heir to the Carlson Brewery fortune, around that time?"

"Yes."

"Did Mr. Carlson propose marriage to Miss Morrow?"

"Yes. Jack Chandler witnessed his proposal at the club."

"Objection, Your Honor! Hearsay!"

"Overruled. I'll allow it."

"Did Mr. Carlson have his family's blessing?"

"Yes."

"Objection, Your Honor! The witness is not privy to that type of information!"

"Sustained. Change your line of questioning, Mrs. Hawkins."

"Your Honor, I plan to show relevance."

"Then, the last question will be stricken from record. Get to the point, Counsel."

"Yes, Your Honor. Mr. Horncastle, did Miss Morrow accept Mr. Carlson's proposal?"

"No. She turned him down."

"Did she tell you this herself?"

"Yes."

"And, what was her reason for passing up an opportunity to marry into an affluent family and enjoy a life of luxury?"

"She said that, if she married for the third time, she wanted to be sure it was for love."

"And she did not love Mr. Carlson?"

"She was not in love with him. She said she wanted him to marry someone who would love him the way he deserved to be loved."

"So, Miss Morrow turned down the opportunity to marry into money?"

"Yes."

"Thank you, Mr. Horncastle. That is all."

Tony's eyes were searing as they riveted on Brett's face. Whispers and a dull hum of shared remarks filled the courtroom as spectators shifted in their creaking seats.

"Call your next witness, Mrs. O'Brien." the judge's voice drowned out the hushed remarks.

"Defense calls Donald Horncastle."

Edna's eyes searched across the courtroom for her sister. As Donald rose from his seat, his dutiful wife, impeccably dressed in a cranberry wool suit and a plastic smile painted on her face, whispered inaudible words of encouragement to him. That smile remained as her eyes followed her husband to the witness box. Edna wondered what it would require to remove it: A blow torch, perhaps. Melting layer by layer, it would expose merely cold wax underneath. On the other side of Annette, Dottie was biting her nails. Beside Dottie, Audrey sat upright and alert.

"Please state your relationship to the defendant."

"I am his older brother."

"Has your brother always lived in the family home with yourself, your other brother, your sister, your spouses and children?"

"Yes. Warren's always lived with us."

"Have any of you observed your brother behave in a discriminatory manner toward women in general?"

"No."

"Have any of the other women he dated ever made allegations of assault or any other type of impropriety?"

"No."

"Not in all the years you have lived under the same roof?"

"Never."

"Would you say your brother has dated a considerable amount of women?"

"Oh, yes. Definitely." Donald smiled, "Warren has a keen eye for beautiful women."

"And, in all this time, no one else has made any type of allegations against him?"

"Not one."

"I understand Miss Goldstein is related to you through marriage."

"Yes. She is my wife's niece."

"The illegitimate daughter of your wife's sister and your childhood friend. Is that right?"

"Yes."

"I understand she was a missing person for most of her life."

"Yes. Edna – that is my wife's sister – was married to another man at the time. He suspected she was not his own child and out of vengeance, following their divorce, he abducted her. He and his new lady friend moved around all the time with the child to cover their tracks.”

“I understand you provided financial assistance for your sister-in-law in her search for her daughter.”

“Yes.”

“The search was unsuccessful. Trained detectives were unable to locate her missing daughter for decades. Then, two and a half years ago, she turned up in Beavertown.”

“Yes.”

“What was your impression of the young woman upon meeting her?”

“Naturally, my wife and I made every effort to be hospitable to her, for Edna and Sid’s sakes. And, initially, Sydney was quite pleasant and charming.”

“How did you feel about your baby brother dating your wife’s niece?”

“We certainly had our qualms. After all, we knew so little about her – where she had been, what she had done, what sort of people she had been involved with.”

“Were you also surprised that your brother had shown an interest in her? Did she seem to be his type?”

“She was not his type at all. He had never shown an interest in Goody Two-Shoes type women before. Sydney was so plain and socially inept, compared to all the glamorous and poised women my brother dated.”

“Were you concerned your brother might break her heart?”

“No. She knew what she was getting into.”

“Why do you think she has accused your brother of rape, Mr. Horncastle?”

“It’s a classic ‘woman scorned’ scenario. When she realized he did not return her feelings, she decided to strike back. Sydney is a very troubled woman. Living in abject poverty most of her life must have affected her in ways we cannot imagine."

"Objection, Your Honor! Speculation!" Kitty intercepted.

"Sustained. Advise your witness to keep to the facts, Mrs. O'Brien."

"No more questions, Your Honor."

"Your witness, Mrs. Hawkins."

Edna glanced at her sister again. She was still smiling.

"Mr. Horncastle, you mentioned earlier that your brother is the baby of the family."

"Yes."

"In fact, he is considerably younger than all of you, is he not? He is closer in age to his nephews than he is to his siblings."

"Yes."

"He was not raised like the rest of you, was he?"

"I'm not sure I understand the question."

"He was given more leeway, indulged more than the four of you, was he not?"

"I suppose so. Our parents were getting on in years and did not have the energy they once had."

"Was your brother frequently in trouble at school?"

"Nothing major."

"What sorts of trouble was he in?"

"Just the usual stuff boys get into...Cutting class, smoking, being rude to teachers."

"Was he not in trouble for luring girls to a secluded place in a wooded area behind the school and offering them cigarettes and alcohol in exchange for sexual favors?"

"Well...er..." his face turned crimson.

"In fact, had he not established his reputation as a playboy even back in his school days?"

"Well...I suppose so."

"Did you or your other brother ever do those things?"

"No, but..."

"Mr. Horncastle, you have two sisters, do you not?"

"Yes."

"Were they ever in trouble when they were growing up?"

"Not Audrey." he glanced at his sister as though seeking her approval.

"Audrey Chandler is your elder sister, am I right?"

"Yes. She was a model student."

"Your other sister: Was she ever in trouble?"

"Yes. Frances often landed herself in some sort of trouble."

"What sorts of trouble did she land herself in?"

"Abusing drugs and alcohol...Prostitution..." his voice trailed off.

"Where is your sister Frances today, Mr. Horncastle?"

"I...I'm not sure."

"A close-knit family like yours, and you don't know the whereabouts of your baby sister?"

"Francie's a free spirit."

"Has she not spent considerable time in addiction treatment centers throughout North America in the past five decades?"

"She's been in rehab once or twice."

"Was she not disowned by the family as a teenager when she was caught engaging in sexual activity behind the school?"

"Yes."

"Your sister was charging the male students for sexual favors in order to support her addiction to barbiturates and alcohol – at a time when such things were unheard of – isn't that right, Mr. Horncastle?"

"Yes. Francie had her troubles."

"Your parents washed their hands off their problem child, did they not?"

"Yes."

"Were they similarly enraged about your brother Warren's escapades?"

"No."

"Why is that, Mr. Horncastle?"

"I'm not sure."

"Was it because they had one set of expectations for a daughter and a totally different one for a son?"

"I'm not sure I understand."

"Were they not practicing a double standard, sending out the message that it was permissible for males to behave irresponsibly, but not so for females?"

"Not particularly."

"Were they not inadvertently sowing the seeds for your brother's callous treatment of women by condoning his bad behavior in his youth?"

"Objection, Your Honor!" Beth sprang up.

"Overruled. I'll grant you some leeway, Mrs. Hawkins, but get to the point."

"Thank you, Your Honor. Mr. Horncastle, when your sister was disowned, where did she go?"

"I'm not sure. She travelled around quite a bit."

"When was the next time you saw her?"

"Twenty-one years later. When she suddenly turned up with a sixteen year-old daughter."

"And, did the family welcome her back with open arms?"

"Well...er..."

"Did they allow her back into the fold?"

"Well...Not exactly."

"Did she remain in Beavertown?"

"No. She just wanted to leave her daughter with us and disappear again."

"Is that what transpired, Mr. Horncastle?"

"Yes."

"Did your family take her daughter in?"

"No."

"Wasn't it your wife's sister Edna Goldstein and her husband, your friend, Sidney Goldstein, who took her in?"

"Well, yes. But, my dad paid her expenses."

"Did she live in your family home?"

"No. Ella lived with Edna and Sid in the guest house, which is on the property."

"And, your sister's daughter, Ella: Did she physically resemble your sister Frances or any other members of your family?"

"Not exactly."

"In fact, your niece, Ella Hendricks was black, was she not?"

An outpouring of shock erupted from the courtroom. The judge's gavel beat out a furious drumbeat, to no avail.

"Order in the courtroom! Order! Please come to order!"

The words were drowned out by the drone of spectators.

"Order!" the judge demanded.

The stunned crowd, once aware of the command, acquiesced.

"Let us proceed."

"Thank you, Your Honor." Kitty, who had been immobilized by the mob of spectators, came back to life, "Did your family ever learn the identity of young Ella's father, Mr. Horncastle?"

"Yes. He was a jazz musician my sister met in Chicago."

"Did he, at any point, make any attempts to see his daughter?"

"He couldn't."

"Why is that, Mr. Horncastle?"

"He was deceased."

"Had he been involved in his daughter's life before his death?"

"No. He and my sister lost custody of Ella when she was a toddler. She was raised in foster care."

"How did Mr. Hendricks die?"

"A heroin overdose."

"Was your sister also addicted to heroin?"

"Yes."

"Was Ella born addicted?"

"Yes."

"She must have had an awful lot of medical needs, a lot of expenses."

"Yes. Dad paid them all."

"Did Ella triumph in overcoming her problems?"

"Yes. Ella grew into a lovely, intelligent, caring young woman. She went to nursing school and received her diploma."

"And, it was your sister-in-law, Edna Goldstein and your childhood friend Sidney Goldstein who nurtured her, is that right?"

"Yes."

"I understand this lovely young woman died in an accident shortly after receiving her diploma. I am deeply sorry."

"Thank you."

"It must have been particularly painful for Mr. and Mrs. Goldstein, seeing as how they had treated her like their own child and grown to love her deeply."

"Yes. Sid and Edna were terribly shaken by Ella's loss."

"When, five years later, they were reunited with their biological daughter, was your entire family happy for them?"

"Of course."

"Were some of you concerned when your brother Warren started dating her?"

"I don't understand."

"Didn't some members of your family express concern that your brother might hurt this newcomer, considering his track record with women?"

"I suppose so."

"In fact, your two nephews, Anthony Horncastle and Jackson Chandler both support the plaintiffs, Miss Goldstein and Miss Morrow, do they not?"

"Yes."

"How many children do you have, Mr. Horncastle?"

"Objection, Your Honor! Relevance!"

"I plan to show relevance, Your Honor."

"Please get to it, Mrs. Hawkins."

"Yes, Your Honor. Please answer the question, Mr. Horncastle."

"Two. My daughter, Dorothy, who is nineteen, and my son, Garrett...thirty-three."

"You had to think about his age first, didn't you, Mr. Horncastle?"

"It's difficult to keep track."

"With only two children, you'd think it would be fairly simple. After all, birthdays are celebrated each year. Cards and gifts are given."

"My son does not live at home."

"Where does he live?"

"I'm not sure."

"Did he leave on friendly terms?"

"No."

"Why is that, Mr. Horncastle?"

"Garrett did not get along too well with the rest of us."

"I see. Was he asked to leave, or did he decide on his own?"

"He was asked to leave." he shifted in his seat.

"How long has it been since he left?"

“Two years.”

“Has he been in contact?”

“No.”

“Why is that?”

“He…er…has troubles.”

“What kind of troubles?”

“Er…legal troubles.”

“What has he been in trouble for in the past, Mr. Horncastle?”

“For possession.”

“Possession of what?”

“Marijuana and LSD.”

“Anything else?”

“Break and Enter.”

“So, he has been convicted of serious crimes. How many break-ins did he commit?”

“Three.” he murmured.

“Homes? Businesses?”

“Homes in the neighborhood.”

“Did he serve prison time?”

“Yes.”

“How many drug convictions does he have?”

“Seven…no, eight.”

“And he served time for those?”

“Yes.”

“He has one other conviction, too, does he not?”

"Yes."

"And, what was that for?"

"...For..." he lowered his voice to a whisper, "...sexual assault..."

"Thank you, Mr. Horncastle. That will be all."

"This court will adjourn until nine a.m. tomorrow." the judge announced.

Donald crossed the courtroom wearily to the reassuring presence of his wife. Dottie fled alone and unnoticed by her family. Audrey and Mildred took turns reassuring Donald and Annette. Willard walked out with Donald, and the three women followed behind. The half-empty courtroom smelled of body odor and mocked Sydney with its hushed voices.

Chapter 10/ Handle With Care

Leaning seductively against the pink column in the far right corner, she took a long drag off her cigarette and tossed back her long brown tresses. She cast an icy glare at Sydney, who was on the stairs.

"Bitch." the younger woman uttered under her breath, flinging her cigarette butt in her direction.

Sydney flinched and quickened her steps. Sweeping past dazed groups congregated in the middle of the hallway, she made her way to the courtroom and took her seat. The doors swung open and spectators trickled in. Diane walked up to the defense table deliberately and lingered before Beth, forcing eye contact.

"Hello, Bethann." she said coldly.

"Hello, Diane." the other woman responded nervously.

Diane regarded her with ice-blue eyes for another instant before resuming her seat.

Judge Clayton returned and wearily announced the continuation. He cast a swift glance at the pale, distraught Sydney as Beth announced:

"Defense calls Celia Emerson."

Sydney froze.

"What is she doing here?" Brett whispered to her.

"Heaven knows."

"I wonder what the bitch has to say."

"Nothing good."

"Don't let her get to you. She'll expose her ignorance and stupidity on the stand. The jury's going to see right through her. I think the judge is sympathetic to us."

"I'm not sure about the jury."

"The jury's full of mothers, who see their daughters in you, their sisters and friends in me."

"Brett, you're my rock."

"I'll tear Celia into shreds when I get my turn to question her." Kitty reassured them.

Celia's pinpoint hazel eyes were riveted on the threesome at the prosecution table, intuitively aware she was the topic of their whispers.

"Mrs. Emerson," Beth attempted to divert her attention, "What community groups are you involved with?"

"I volunteer at the Rape Crisis Center."

"Then, you come into contact with women who have been sexually assaulted."

"Yes. On a regular basis. I spend considerable time counselling them and listening to them, and basically holding their hands."

"And, did either Miss Goldstein or Miss Morrow ever seek help at the Rape Crisis Center?"

"No."

"You know Miss Goldstein from the university, do you not?"

"Yes. We have been study companions."

"Then, you had contact with her following her alleged attack?"

"Yes. We prepared for our exams together."

"Did Miss Goldstein display any behavior consistent with women who have been victims of sexual assault?"

"Objection!" Kitty protested, "Speculation!"

"Your Honor, Mrs. Emerson has some expertise in this field. Her opinion would be an educated, well-informed one."

"I'll allow it."

"Please answer the question, Mrs. Emerson." Beth said.

"Nothing in her behavior indicated she had been sexually assaulted. She did not behave any differently than usual."

"Has Miss Goldstein ever confided in you regarding her personal life?"

"Not so much. But from our general conversations, I was able to tell she feels quite a bit of hostility toward men."

"Did she ever talk about Mr. Horncastle or any other man in her life?"

"She did not talk about her relationships, however, I had occasion to observe her at her place of work. It was quite apparent she had an immature school-girl crush on her employer, Mr. Chandler. Sydney has a dependent personality. She is not able to form healthy relationships with men. She has deep-seated issues regarding her sexuality."

"Please be more explicit, Mrs. Emerson."

"Miss Goldstein is attracted more to women than she is to men. She has an unhealthy relationship with her colleague, Miss Morrow. She is smothering her with her constant need for attention."

"Objection!" Kitty sprang to her feet, "Defense is wasting the Court's time with childish speculation!"

Brett held Sydney's forearm to prevent her from bolting out of her seat to strangle Celia.

"Your Honor," Beth responded nonchalantly, "My witness is trained to make assessments regarding people's mental health."

"Prosecution is right. Change your line of questioning, Mrs. O'Brien."

"No more questions, Your Honor. Your witness, Mrs. Hawkins."

Kitty strode up with deliberate steps.

"Mrs. Emerson, you claim to be an expert in human behavior, yet all you have produced here are dime-store Pop Psychology theories steeped in old, worn-out clichés and sweeping generalizations."

"I am a trained professional. I have a private practice."

"So you say. And, apparently, the misinformed, misguided citizens of Beavertown believe you. What degree do you currently hold, Mrs. Emerson?"

"I'm working on my Master's Degree in Educational Counselling."

"Working on." she cut her off briskly, "What degree have you actually completed, Mrs. Emerson?"

"Bachelor of Arts." she stated, squirming in her seat.

"I see. Where did you receive your Bachelor of Arts degree?"

"St. Matthew's University."

"Not East Coast University? Why S.M.U.?"

"It's a smaller, friendlier university."

"Or is it because you were refused admission to E.C.U. because your qualifications did not meet their considerably higher standards?"

"I chose S.M.U. because of the atmosphere."

"Really? Even though you were aware that a Bachelor of Arts degree from S.M.U. is not as marketable as a degree from E.C.U.?"

"S.M.U. is a perfectly good institution." she retorted.

"What degree did you apply for at E.C.U. following your graduation from S.M.U.?"

"Master of Arts."

"Were you accepted?"

"No...But..."

"When you received your degree, what were your grades?"

"Straight A's." she stated with her chin tilted up.

"And, were you not told those A's were worth only C's by E.C.U. standards?"

"Yes."

"Did you have to do something in order to qualify for graduate work?"

"Yes. I had to enroll in the Bachelor of Education program and apply for a Master of Education degree after completion. I have been doing other things during the course of my Bachelor of Education degree: I am licensed in Reality Therapy. I've had a private practice since receiving my certification in Reality Therapy."

"Yes. I'm familiar with the one-weekend accreditation, the instant certificate in a simplistic new method. And that led you to believe you were qualified to help people?"

"I am qualified."

"Mrs. Emerson," Kitty stood facing her squarely in the eyes, "You have expressed strong antagonism toward Miss Goldstein. What has she done to hurt you?"

"I...don't understand."

"What has Miss Goldstein done to make you feel so resentful?"

"Nothing."

"In fact, she has been more than obliging and generous, has she not, always sharing books and articles that might be of use to you in your work?"

"Yes."

"So, this is a woman who has extended her friendship to you, has been gracious and kind, yet you speak so disparagingly about her?"

"That is nonsense." she retorted in indignation.

"You have done absolutely nothing to reciprocate her generosity. In fact, you have been an adversary under the guise of friendship, have you not?"

"No. I've always tried to help Sydney."

"Help yourself is more like it. You've used her resources, taken advantage of her generosity, used her as your lab rat...Now you're here, making malicious, uninformed claims about her. Have you not, in fact, attempted to undermine her confidence in herself, found constant fault with her?"

"Constructive criticism is necessary in the healing process."

"Sydney Goldstein is considerably younger than yourself, by fifteen years, is she not? She is also quite a stunning woman. You are envious of her youth and beauty, are you not, Mrs. Emerson? She reminds you of all your missed opportunities. You do not want her to have the things you did not have at her age. You resent her success at university, her integrity, and the personal strength she displays in all of her dealings. You are, indeed, competitive with her, aren't you?"

"I have no reason to feel competitive or envious." Celia snickered under her breath, "Sydney has nothing I could ever want. She is a very troubled, insecure woman. She is lonely, bitter and needy."

"Miss Goldstein has displayed a quiet dignity in the face of great adversity. Knowing deep down that she possesses such inner resources must be intimidating. You've led a life of privilege, have you not, Mrs. Emerson? A military doctor's daughter, a colonel's wife…You look at Miss Goldstein, who was raised in abject poverty with no family to care for her. You wonder how it is that she has survived. You cannot begin to imagine how you could surmount the obstacles she has."

"Sydney is a very sick person. When people grow up in the type of environment she has, they cannot become fully functioning human beings. She's delusional. This entire rape thing is a figment of her imagination. She has misunderstood Warren Horncastle and now destroyed the teaching career he worked so hard to build."

"You say there was no rape. Yet, there's physical evidence, Mrs. Emerson. Now, who's delusional?"

"I am not saying there was no sexual activity. But I have no doubt, it was consensual. Sydney is needy."

"Was her miscarriage also consensual?"

"Warren Horncastle did not know she was pregnant. She ought to have known not to engage in rough, kinky sex in her condition. She has no right to blame him. She was careless and irresponsible."

"So, you think she deserved what happened to her?"

"She had to face the consequences of her actions."

"I see. So you are saying the victim is to blame."

"Sydney is not a victim. There was no crime committed here. She had sex with her on-again-off-again lover. It's ludicrous to cry rape when it's someone she has slept with willingly in the past."

"But, in this instance, she said 'no', and he forced himself on her."

"He was entitled to those privileges. They had been dating."

"So, you're saying it is acceptable for a man to have his way with a woman who says 'no', if she has willingly slept with him before?"

"Yes. They had been a couple. He enjoyed certain privileges. She had no right to withdraw them arbitrarily."

"And you work at the Rape Crisis Center?" Kitty shook her head in exasperation, "That is all. No more questions."

Brett patted Sydney's knee.

"She makes my blood boil." Kitty remarked as she returned to the table, "But, actually, her testimony helps us. She showed her ignorance and incompetence. In this day and age, such blatant victim-blaming is unacceptable."

"She's so smug." Sydney said.

"She's a sick lady." Kitty said.

"With people like her in helping professions, our society is doomed."

"You're right, Sydney. It blows my mind. Anybody off the street with a M.Ed. can hang up their shingle and call themselves a counsellor; then they can go on to mess with people's minds."

"Your Honor," Beth's grating voice drowned out the drone of the spectators, "Defense calls its final witness: Warren Horncastle."

Warren swaggered up to the witness box and was sworn in. His mane appeared to have been shorn and tamed for the occasion. His cobalt blue Italian suit was cut to emphasize and enhance his ample physical assets. The women on the jury were not immune to his blatant sexuality. He glanced over at Sydney, smirked and winked.

"Mr. Horncastle," Beth stood before him, taking in his obvious attractiveness, "You and Miss Goldstein dated between the spring and late fall of 1976. Is that right?"

"That is right."

"Who initiated the contact?"

"I did."

"And, was that because of your overwhelming attraction to her?"

"No. She was not my type. I would not have given Sydney a second glance under normal circumstances."

"Then, why did you approach her?"

"When my nephew Jack hired her, he thought she might be Sid and Edna Goldstein's missing daughter. Jack had to go on tour, so he was not able to look into it himself. My other nephew Tony attempted to get some information from Brett Morrow, however, had no luck. I thought I might have some luck extracting information from the mystery woman herself if I became better acquainted with her and earned her trust."

"Why did you feel compelled to extract this information? Why didn't you wait for her to approach the Goldsteins, if she was their daughter?"

"My family was concerned she might be an imposter: She might have heard about the missing woman and taken on her identity. We thought the real Sydney might be dead or still missing. We were concerned this stranger might be out to extort money and we did not want the Goldsteins to be hurt."

"And, were you able to extract information, as you had hoped?"

"No. She was extremely guarded and tight-lipped."

"Did she make any attempt to contact the Goldsteins?"

"No."

"How was her identity eventually revealed?"

"She confided in Brett Morrow, who arranged a reunion with her parents."

"And, was she who she claimed to be?"

"It all checked out."

"Did you stop seeing her once her identity became known?"

"It wasn't straight forward. Her family and mine are very close and I would have risked causing a rift between our families, were I to break it off abruptly."

"So you continued seeing her, for the sake of maintaining peace between the families?"

"Pretty well."

"Was Miss Goldstein aware of this?"

"No. She thought we were an item." he snickered.

"Did you have a monogamous relationship?"

"I never led her to believe such a thing was or would ever be a possibility with us."

"But she assumed there was some sort of commitment in your relationship?"

"She misunderstood. Sydney was not very bright." he smirked.

"Objection! Inflammatory!" Kitty protested.

"Sustained. Mrs. O'Brien, instruct your witness to keep the commentary to himself and just stick to the questions."

"Yes, Your Honor. Mr. Horncastle, you continued dating other women during the time she believed you were an item?"

"Naturally."

"Did she suspect anything?"

"No." he laughed.

"During this time, did you notice Miss Goldstein becoming too clingy and emotionally demanding?"

"Objection, Your Honor! Counsel is leading the witness!"

"Sustained. Rephrase your question, Mrs. O'Brien."

"What was Miss Goldstein's behavior while you were dating?"

"She was smothering me. I couldn't breathe."

"Yet, you still did not break it off with her?"

"I didn't want her freaking out and running in tears to her Mommy and Daddy."

"Yet, in effect, she did do precisely that, did she not?"

"Yes. I had no idea how deranged the chick was."

"Objection, Your Honor!"

"Sustained. I don't want to remind you again, Mrs. O'Brien."

"Yes, Your Honor. Mr. Horncastle, how did you attempt to resolve the problem with her clinginess?"

"I tried talking to her a number of times, but she became so upset every time, I dropped the subject."

"On the night in question, you showed up at Goldstein's Music Shop to see Miss Goldstein. What was the purpose of your visit?"

"To clear the air and reach some sort of amicable solution."

"And was Miss Goldstein willing to do that?"

"No. She was pressuring me to commit to her."

"What happened on that fateful night, Mr. Horncastle?"

"We argued. I told Sydney I did not want to be tied down. She became terribly upset and said I would be sorry; she would make me pay for rejecting her."

Sydney furrowed her brow and whispered in Kitty's ear.

"He's lying! He's distorting the whole thing!"

"Don't worry. I'll trip him up." Kitty whispered back.

"What did you do, Mr. Horncastle? How did you respond?"

"I didn't take her seriously. I realize now that was a mistake."

"Objection, Your Honor!"

"Sustained. Try to control your witness, Mrs. O'Brien."

"Yes, Your Honor. What transpired next, Mr. Horncastle?"

"I tried to smoothe things over. She seemed to come around and see reason. I thought she was bluffing initially, when she threatened me, so, when she seemed to come around, I believed everything was all right."

"Why do you think she's claiming you raped her?"

"Obviously, she was still resentful about being rejected. I thought she understood the nature of our arrangement, but, apparently, she felt bitter because I was not willing to make a commitment."

"Mr. Horncastle, did you have sexual intercourse with Sydney Goldstein on the evening in question?"

"Yes. We had sex." he smirked, "She initiated it, too. She thought she could change my mind by luring me to have sex."

"Miss Goldstein incurred some injuries. Can you tell the court how she received those injuries?"

"She liked rough, kinky sex. She was so grateful for the attention, she was eager to please – if you know what I mean. She would try just about anything in bed. She injured herself during wild, passionate sex."

"How did she fall and suffer a miscarriage?"

"After we had sex, she started pressuring me for a commitment again. I told her she was no longer attractive to me. She had let herself go and put on weight. I was repulsed. She became very angry, started shouting, stepped back, tripped and fell.”

“She has claimed you refused to get medical help for her when she miscarried. How do you respond to that accusation?”

“I offered to get help for her, but she refused. She said she was having heavy irregular periods, and she had it under control. I did not know she was having a miscarriage.”

“Why do you think she has accused you of rape?”

“Out of vengeance, because I refused to get tricked into marriage. I outsmarted her and called her bluff.”

“Miss Goldstein claims the two of you had a conversation regarding the paternity of her baby following her miscarriage that evening. Would you like to address that?”

“It most certainly was not that evening. She did not inform me of her miscarriage that evening. She approached me several days later and threw it in my face.”

“Did she tell you the child was not yours?”

“Yes, but who was going to believe her? I had no doubt it was mine. What a way to find out!”

“Then, you are certain Miss Goldstein concocted the story about the one-night stand in Toronto?”

“Sydney, have a one-night stand? That is laughable! That little prude, go into a bar and pick up a stranger? Not a chance. She’s afraid of her own shadow. She could never have the nerve, or the finesse. Besides, who’d ever sleep with Sydney, anyway?”

“Some may wonder why you did, Mr. Horncastle. Could you clarify it for the Court, please?”

“I’ve already explained all that. And, I did feel sorry for her. She was so eager to please – like a puppy dog.”

“Your Honor, I object!”

“Sustained. Mrs. O’Brien, you have been duly warned.”

"Yes, Your Honor. Mr. Horncastle, then, you are certain the child she was carrying was yours?"

"Absolutely. She was going to stick me with child support payments if she couldn't get me to marry her. One way or another, she was determined to get me."

"But she lost the baby. She could not get you for support payments. How did she deal with that?"

"She needed another strategy – and accusing me of rape was the most convenient one. You know what they say about a woman scorned."

Unrest among the spectators was making it impossible to follow the proceedings.

"This Court will adjourn for a ten minute recess." Judge Clayton announced.

"Come on, sweetheart. Let's go outside for some air." Brett urged Sydney.

She obliged silently. Brett linked her arm through hers and led her to the pink columns. They sat on the marble ledge.

"No one's taking that asshole seriously." Brett said, "People now see him for what he is."

"I'm sorry for putting you through all this, Brett."

"It's okay, hon. Diane'll get him eventually. Have no fear."

"Beth is going to ask him about you after the recess. I'm so sorry you have to sit there and listen to him."

"I can take it. I have strong shoulders. Come on. Let's go back in and hear what the bastard has to say." she led her back to the courtroom.

With formalities dispensed and the Beth and Warren plastic figurines in place, the proceedings resumed.

"Mr. Horncastle, you have enlightened the Court regarding Miss Goldstein's motives for making these accusations against you. Now, let us go on to the circumstances regarding Miss Morrow. Could you shed some light on her motives for accusing you of rape, as well?"

"Brett's never been a big fan of mine. Particularly since I exposed her scam to get her hands on the Horncastle fortune."

"Objection! Inflammatory!"

"I don't want to have to remind you again, Mrs. O'Brien!"

"Yes, Your Honor. Tell the Court, if you will, why Miss Morrow would wish to extract revenge from you."

"Brett had her hooks into my nephew, Tony. I put a stop to her plans to marry into the family by exposing her sordid life. She never let me forget it, either. Each time our paths crossed, she had some disparaging remarks for me."

"Why do you think she attempted to break up your relationship with Miss Goldstein?"

"She wanted Sydney for herself." he said smugly.

"Objection, Your Honor!"

"Sustained. Mrs. O'Brien, control your witness."

"Did the animosity between you and Miss Morrow escalate during the time you and Miss Goldstein were dating?"

"It certainly did. Brett was obsessed. She was constantly badgering me to leave her precious Sydney alone, telling Sydney lies about me."

"In the early hours of July 11, 1977, why did you go to Chandler's after closing time?"

"To talk to Sydney and find out why she had told Brett I had assaulted her when it wasn't true. Brett had lit into me soon following the incident in December, and made accusations against me. I was sick of being portrayed as the bad guy. Edna and Sid were snubbing me and claiming I had broken their daughter's heart."

"Had Miss Goldstein told them you had assaulted her?"

"Not at that time. She must have told them I dumped her."

"So, you wanted to talk to Miss Goldstein to reach an amicable solution and end the animosity?"

"Yes. I wanted to move on without constant reproach. I wanted her to move on with her life, as well."

"When you arrived at Chandler's, what did you find?"

"Sydney wasn't there. Brett was alone."

"What took place?"

"At first, she berated me for hurting her precious Sydney. She had been drinking heavily. Then, she asked me to help her unzip her gown so she could change into her casual clothes."

"What did you do?"

"I obliged. But she didn't seem to want me to leave. She was desperate for some male companionship. I told her I had to go, but she pleaded with me to stay."

"And, did she persuade you to stay?"

"Well...Brett is a very sexy chick...What can I say? She kissed me...tried to cajole me...I was trying to get away, but after all, there's only so much restraint a guy can exercise in the face of such temptation."

"Mr. Horncastle, did you have sexual intercourse with Miss Morrow that night?"

"I certainly did. And, she was more than willing. When an alluring woman throws herself at you, what is a guy to do?" he turned his boyish charm on the jury.

"Why do you think Miss Morrow is accusing you of rape?"

"Her guilty conscience. She admonished Sydney for sleeping with me, but she jumped in the sack with me herself once Sydney was out of the picture. How was she going to explain that to Sydney? Sydney would never forgive her, so she concocted the rape story. This also gives her the opportunity to even the score with me for breaking up her relationship with my nephew.”

“Thank you, Mr. Horncastle. Your witness, Mrs. Hawkins.”

Sydney’s hand was tightly clasped around Brett’s. With her other hand, she tenderly wiped a tear from Brett’s cheek.

“Mr. Horncastle,” Kitty stood before him, “You stated earlier that your family was initially concerned Miss Goldstein might be an imposter and you jumped at the chance to expose her, if such was the case, or to be the hero by reuniting her with her biological parents if she was, indeed, Sydney Goldstein, the missing woman.”

“I wanted to be helpful.”

“You said she had not come forward to approach the Goldsteins. If she had been an imposter, would she not have been eager to make immediate contact with them?”

“I suppose so. She also might have been playing coy. The possibilities were endless.”

“So, you decided to make a great personal sacrifice and date a woman who was not your type. Is that right?”

“I was willing to do whatever was necessary to find out who she was and what she wanted.”

“So, you felt the best method for extracting information from a woman was seduction?”

“Hey, if it works.”

“And, did Miss Goldstein succumb to your charms?”

“She certainly did.” he glanced at Sydney, “She was pretty easy pickings. She was a bashful, timid wallflower. The attention blew her away.”

“You must have found it exciting to be dating a woman of mystery.”

“It was no big deal.”

"And, did she reveal to you, after you seduced her, that she was, indeed, Sydney Goldstein?"

"No."

"In fact she confided in Miss Morrow, did she not?"

"Yes."

"You must have been disappointed, Mr. Horncastle, that after you had gone to such trouble to spend time with a woman you did not find attractive, making personal sacrifices to win her heart, that she had trusted Miss Morrow more."

"I didn't care."

"Mr. Horncastle, do you think it's ethical to mislead someone and sleep with them, just to get information from them?"

"It's not against the law."

"No. It's not against the law, but it is against decency; it is against humanity. It's repugnant."

"Hey, the chick was lonely. It was like leading a lamb to slaughter. I hardly had to do anything to twist her arm. Like I said, she was easy pickings."

"And, that makes it all right?"

"She was a grown woman. She knew what she was getting into. She played with fire and got burned. There's no one to blame except herself. Sydney's the one who made a fool of herself. Besides, there's no law against it."

"No. There's no law against playing with another person's emotions and taking advantage of their loneliness. Callousness is not illegal, but it is unethical."

"Objection, Your Honor! My colleague's badgering the witness!"

"Sustained. Change your line of questioning, Mrs. Hawkins."

"Yes, Your Honor. Mr. Horncastle, you've given your account of the events on the evening of December 10th, 1976. You claim you did not realize she was having a miscarriage until several days later."

"That is correct."

"And, when you found out, you were angry, because you believed yourself to be the father of her unborn child and considered her pregnancy to be a scheme to either press you for a commitment, or get you to pay child support. Is that right?"

"That was obvious."

"In fact, Mr. Horncastle, did you not say: 'If she couldn't get me one way, she was determined to get me another way.'?"

"That's right."

"Then, you must have been relieved that Miss Goldstein miscarried."

"Objection, Your Honor!"

"Sustained. Please change your line of questioning, Counsel."

"Yes, Your Honor." Kitty inhaled deeply, "Mr. Horncastle, do you expect this Court to believe that, Miss Goldstein initiated rigorous sexual activity with you when she was three months pregnant and later refused your offer of medical help when she began to bleed profusely?"

"Those are the facts."

"And, why do you suppose Miss Goldstein insists to this day the child she was carrying was not yours? If she had been after commitment or child support, would she not have informed you of her pregnancy earlier? Would she not have told you the child was yours?"

"Sydney's a strange chick. She does not do things like other people." he snickered, "Besides, the child was dead. It wouldn't have done her any good to tell me it was mine."

"A woman would tell the father of her lost child it was his." Kitty said sharply.

"Maybe she was playing some sort of a game, trying to make me jealous." he laughed.

"A miscarriage is hardly an occasion for making someone jealous." she retorted, "Now, let's move ahead to the early hours of July 11th, 1977. What was the purpose of your late night visit to your nephew's jazz lounge?"

"To talk to Sydney and see if we could work something out."

"I thought you were glad to be free of her."

"Yes I was."

"For someone so anxious to break up with one's lover, you seem to have gone to great lengths to 'work things out', resolve problems and reach amicable solutions, Mr. Horncastle. Why wouldn't you simply move on and forget about your former lover once the relationship had dissolved?"

"I felt sorry for her, you know. I wanted to help her out."

"Help her in what way?"

"Get her some counselling."

"And, this conversation could not be held during regular hours?"

"I'm pretty busy. It was the only spare time I had."

"When you realized Miss Goldstein was not there – in fact, no one except Miss Morrow was there, did you leave?"

"I attempted to, but Brett detained me." he smirked.

"Yes. She was overcome with lust at the sight of you."

"I cannot help that. Some of us have what it takes."

"Mr. Horncastle, you've made it clear you do not have any respect for women." a frustrated Kitty said, her face flushed.

"Objection, Your Honor!" Beth's voice was lacklustre.

"Overruled. I'll allow it."

"Mr. Horncastle, have you ever been married?"

"No."

"Thank God for that."

"Objection!"

"No more questions." Kitty walked away wearily.

Judge Clayton called a ten minute recess. Brett and Sydney embraced. Edna and Marin came up to them to provide comfort. Jack and Tony hesitantly joined them. Words were not necessary. As Court reconvened, Kitty took her place before the jury to deliver her concluding remarks.

"Your Honor, ladies and gentlemen of the jury, my colleague: Warren Horncastle is a predator who, by his own admission, uses women for his own pleasure and convenience. He is a callous, calculating man. He saw nothing wrong with seducing Miss Goldstein in order to procure information from her. When she realized she was being exploited and attempted to end the relationship, she paid a high price. Mr. Horncastle wanted to have the upper hand, as always, and was enraged that a woman would actually say 'no' to him. He wanted to 'put her in her place'. When Miss Goldstein asserted herself – something a woman is not permitted to do in a relationship with him – she was brutally raped and lost the child she was carrying. Rape is not an act of desire; it is about power. It's a man's way of exerting his power over a woman, of humiliating and demeaning her. Mr. Horncastle displayed wanton disregard for her life when he left her hemorrhaging and alone, refused to seek medical help for her despite her pleas because he believed the child she was miscarrying was his."

Warren sat at the Defense table, shaking his head in disbelief, a crooked grin still affixed to his face.

"Mr. Horncastle then decided to exact revenge on Miss Morrow, who he believed to be responsible for his losing Miss

Goldstein. Mr. Horncastle is unable to deal with rejection. He has enjoyed a loose and free lifestyle all these years, without having to face the consequences of his boorish behavior. Until now, he had not met a woman who was able to resist his charms. Miss Goldstein's need for self-preservation drove her away from the heartless man who had no regard for her. Mr. Horncastle was unable to comprehend that a woman would possess the self-respect and inner strength to end an ongoing relationship which was unhealthy and to face being alone. Her composure was a blow to his ego. In fact, Miss Goldstein has maintained her composure throughout this entire ordeal. Mr. Horncastle is a misogynist and a morally bankrupt man who is a threat to other women, as well."

Beth was furiously writing and whispering to Warren. Kitty made a conscious effort to meet her gaze.

"He harbored deep feelings of resentment for Miss Morrow, who is an independent, forthright woman who could see beyond his veneer and call his bluff. Not only did she not have a romantic interest in him, but she was blunt with him when she felt he was out of line, and she joked with him, which irritated and infuriated him. When he reached his boiling point, he released all his pent-up rage against her in a depraved act. Defense has failed to show any plausible explanation for what happened on December 10th 1976, and July 11th 1977. Without a shadow of a doubt, Mr. Horncastle did, indeed, rape Sydney Goldstein and Brett Morrow. Furthermore, he has shown no remorse for his actions. You must find him guilty of these heinous acts and provide some degree of compensation for his victims. Thank you."

Edna smiled. Her eyes followed Kitty back to her seat. Her compassion, her eloquence spread a warmth in her chest. Beth strode up: Cumbersome, imposing, inelegant, single-minded...

"Your Honor, ladies and gentlemen of the jury, my colleague: There is, indeed, a victim here today: A victim of revenge, envy, and heartless manipulation by two mentally unstable women. Warren Horncastle has been publicly humiliated; he has lost his good standing in the community, his teaching career, the respect of his colleagues. Yes, Warren Horncastle is the only victim here. Sydney Goldstein is a desperate, clingy woman who is too socially inept to attract men. She is a deeply troubled woman who fantasized about a life with an affluent and handsome man like Mr. Horncastle, and was unable to accept reality when he told her a future for them was out of the question. He had grown tired of her dependency and tried to break off their relationship, however, she was hopelessly in love with him, and in a last-ditch effort to hang on to him, she threw herself at him. He saw through her scheme of getting pregnant to rope him into marriage and refused to be taken in. Miss Goldstein retaliated by blaming him for the miscarriage and claiming that he had raped her. Later, she and Miss Morrow concocted a scheme to make my client pay for breaking Miss Goldstein's heart. When Miss Morrow crossed paths with him, she lured him into having sexual intercourse with her, in order to bolster up the false accusations they were building against him. She knew he had a weakness for women and she used her feminine wiles to get him into bed, so she could claim she, too, had been raped. Miss Morrow is well-known for being indiscriminate in her choice of partners. She has a voracious sexual appetite. Mr. Horncastle does not need to take any woman against her will when he has a bevy of willing and amorous women waiting in the wings. This entire case is a waste of the Court's time. It's a blatant attempt at retaliation by a spurned lover. The only thing Miss Goldstein is the victim of is unrequited love. The last time I checked, it was not a crime. Please do not allow these vengeful women to get away with this. My client has already suffered irreparable damage. It would be a great miscarriage of justice to believe these lies. Prosecution has failed to prove there was anything but consensual sex between my client and both of his accusers. He is innocent of any wrongdoing. That is why you must deliver a verdict of 'not guilty', and end this travesty imposed on him by two vicious women. Thank you."

"This Court will adjourn until one p.m. tomorrow, at which time we shall hear the jury's verdict. Court is dismissed."

Spectators filed out in small groups, humming like hornets.

"Lunch?" Jack tapped her on the shoulder.

"I would love to." she said brightly.

Concealing their love from everyone – even her parents – was painful but necessary. His arm found its way around her shoulder as he led her outside.

* * *

Jack's long blond eyelashes were bejewelled with raindrops. He took her arm and held the black umbrella over her head, leaving his own head unprotected as they quickened their steps along Queen Street toward the courthouse.

Once in the building, they came apart to be inconspicuous.

The jury was ready to deliver their verdict.

"Mr. Chairman, has the jury reached its verdict?" Judge Clayton asked.

"Yes, Your Honor, we have." a stocky, balding man in a plaid polyester suit responded.

"On the count of rape against Sydney Goldstein, how does the jury find the defendant, Warren Horncastle?"

"Not Guilty, Your Honor."

"On the count of rape against Brett Morrow, how do you find the defendant?"

"Not Guilty, Your Honor."

In the flurry of activity that followed, Warren beamed and shook Beth's hand. He then glanced back first at Brett, then at Sydney, his coal-black eyes scorching her. Brett collapsed into Sydney's arms.

"It's going to be all right, Sydney." Jack reassured her, "Diane's going to see to it he gets what he deserves."

"I always expected this outcome, but a part of me kept hoping against hope that justice would prevail."

"It will, in the end. You have to have faith."

"Jack is right, darling." Edna kissed her.

"Thank you."

"Let's go home, dear."

"Please go ahead without me, Mom, Dad. Brett please go with them, too, honey. I need to take a walk to clear my head."

"Are you sure you'll be all right?"

"I'm sure. I'll see all of you later."

"I'll stay with her." Jack said.

He led her away, to their own safe cocoon. She knew no one could harm her now because Jack was hers and nothing else mattered.

Chapter 11/ Winter Rhapsody

Warren surveyed his surroundings with bemused detachment. The battle-worn apartment flaunted its gaudy blue paint, cracked plaster, rotting window frames and blackened hardwood floors with metal heat grates.

"So, this is your new digs."

"You like?" she stood by the window in her scoop-neck tee and tight mini skirt.

"Not bad. It has character." he sat on the scarlet red loveseat, "I see you got to keep all the furniture. You've done well for yourself there, Miss Linda."

"When he was on tour, he gave me carte blanche to buy whatever I wanted for the apartment and charge it to his credit card. We were planning to share the rest of our lives. I'm not the one who broke that promise. He has to keep paying rent on the old place until April or break the lease. Whatever he does, it's not my responsibility or concern anymore. He's only getting what he deserves."

"I wouldn't want to get on your bad side, Linda. You're a dangerous woman."

"No one gets to break off his engagement to me and get away with it."

"I think you got that point across to him loud and clear." he crossed his legs, "I saw you outside the courthouse day in and day out, haranguing the poor schnook. Just return the man's property, Linda. What purpose does it serve to hang on to his high school yearbooks and athletic trophies?"

"He didn't take them with him when he cleared out his stuff."

"He couldn't take them because you had hidden them."

"What is this sudden affection for your nephew? I thought you couldn't stand him."

"Your 'poor me' routine is starting to sound like a bad country song, Linda. Give this a break."

"I want him back."

"Why do you want someone who doesn't want you?"

"I don't want her to get her hooks into him."

"You're overestimating her. I didn't pick up on anything between them during the court proceedings. She was fawning all over Brett the whole time."

The amber bubble-dome stereo was playing Van McCoy's "Love Is The Answer". Warren stretched and yawned.

"I won't have any peace of mind as long as that Stanley chick is working there with him. I want her gone."

"Her name is Sydney and I don't see her leaving any time soon."

"Hey, whose side are you on here?" she threw a fringed cotton cushion at him.

"What do you think?" he smirked.

"I want to fuck up her life."

"Her life's already fucked up, Linda."

"If she makes one move on him, I'll show her. If she takes away what I love, I'll take away what she loves." she stood hovering over him.

"Give this a rest. You're killing the mood. I came here for some afternoon delight and you're giving me all this bullshit. I don't have the time or the patience for any of this, Linda."

"I thought you'd want to see her suffer."

"She's already suffered. I've moved on. I suggest you do the same."

"She's a problem that needs to be dealt with. I have my ways of taking out the trash."

"That's enough talk. Now, let's get down to some business." he stood and pinched her rump.

She laughed with demonic delight. Her eyes ablaze, she wrapped her arms around his neck.

* * *

She tucked her head into his armpit and inhaled his masculine scent. It made her feel safe and protected. This was her sanctuary. She belonged here. She ran her fingers through the wheat fields of hair on his chest. He stirred and mumbled in his sleep. Blond eyelashes fluttered against his smooth cheeks. Feeling her soft kiss on his chest, he opened his eyes.

"Sydney, honey, you're awake."

"I just woke up."

"I still can't believe I'm lucky enough to wake up to your beautiful face every morning for the rest of my life."

"I'm the lucky one."

"There's no one like you, Sydney. I wasn't alive until I met you." he kissed her hand and pressed it to his cheek.

"You're the one who gave me life, Jack."

"Sydney, I've made a decision I want to share with you."

"What is it?"

"There'll be no more tours from now on. Jack Chandler is retiring from the music industry."

"But, Jack...That's your life, your passion."

"You're my life, my passion now."

"Are you sure about this?"

"I'm sick of that superficial lifestyle and all the trappings that go with it. I want something real, something fulfilling – and that is only possible with you. There's something else. When Tony and Brett join us in John's Bay to be our witnesses, he's going to bring all the paperwork to finalize it: Your name is going to be added as an owner. You and I are going to own twenty-five percent each of Chandler's."

"Jack, are you sure about this? All I want or need is your love. Material things are not important to me."

"You're going to be my wife, my life partner. I also want you to be my business partner."

She kissed both his hands and held them against her tear-streaked cheeks.

"Being able to tell my parents, Brett and Tony after the trial ended and getting their blessings felt so good after having to sneak around and hide in this hotel to keep our relationship a secret from everyone."

"Keeping my distance from you during the trial was sheer torture."

"For me, too."

"Hiding out in this hotel room the whole time was kind of fun, though, wasn't it?"

"I have to admit, it was."

"We've got a long day ahead of us tomorrow, sweetheart. You'll need your sleep. It's three-ten now. We should try to catch another three or four hours of sleep."

"I'm too excited to sleep."

"I'll give you a sleeping pill." he winked, sliding the covers off her, "I want to start and end each day by making love to you." He raised himself on his elbow.

"I think that can be arranged." she held his face in her hands.

His lips planted tender kisses on her eyelids, her nose, cheek, and slid down to her lips. She guided him on top of her. His tongue, his lips, his fingertips awakened every nerve ending in her body. Filled with his sweet nectar, she cradled him in her arms. Spent and vulnerable, he opened his eyes and looked up at her.

"Sydney, don't ever leave me, please!"

"I'll never leave you, Jack."

Those eyes. Those eyes had captivated her from the moment she had met him that fateful spring day in 1976. She had never imagined she would be lying in his arms. She had never imagined he, too, would want her.

* * *

"I love you so much, sweetheart." her dad's arms pulled her down and pressed her to his chest.

"I love you, too, Dad." she kissed his cheek.

"It makes me so proud, so happy to see my beautiful daughter marry her handsome prince. This is a dream come true for your mom and me." He kissed her forehead.

"Thank you, Dad."

"I know you'll take good care of my little girl, Jack." her dad shook Jack's hand.

"I promise, sir."

"My baby, this is such a happy day." Edna kissed Sydney on both cheeks, "I love you, my sweet girl."

"I love you so much, Mom." she kissed her.

"Thank you, Tony, for driving us here to share our baby's wedding day."

"It was my pleasure, Edna." Tony patted her arm.

Jack shook hands with Edna.

"Congratulations, sweetheart! I'm so happy for you!" Brett embraced Sydney.

"Thank you for being here, Brett. I love you."

"I love you, hon. I'm honored to be sharing this with you."

"Thank you, Tony." Sydney shook his hand.

"You're welcome, Sydney. Enjoy your night, buddy." Tony winked at Jack.

"Drive safely." Jack called out after them, with an arm around Sydney, "Well, Mrs. Chandler, now we're official."

He held up her hand: A single carat solitaire diamond mounted on an unadorned platinum band and a matching wedding band were Sydney's choice. He had offered to buy her larger, more expensive rings – the sky was the limit, he had told her – yet, she had chosen understated elegance over ostentatious, vulgar garishness. Even her choice of dress was a classic beaded, mid-length one with simple lines and a curve-enhancing bias cut. Her white fascinator was a tasteful option for the civil ceremony. Her shoes were medium-heeled and feminine. She and Brett had selected her wedding attire at the high-end family-owned Kulp's department store across the town square from their hotel.

Their dinner for six at the hotel restaurant following the ceremony at City Hall had been a warm, intimate one shared with their loved ones. He had booked the piano bar for their private listening and dancing pleasure. Edna and Sid had watched with pride as the two younger couples had danced to the songs Jack had requested – Sydney's favorites: "My One And Only Love", "I Didn't Know What Time It Was", "Long Ago And Far Away", "All The Things You Are", "You're Nearer", "You're My World", and a wide assortment of Gershwin songs. Now, they were ready for private time in their suite with a bottle of champagne. He led her to the elevator with an arm around her. Sydney was his, at long last. Sydney, the woman he had dreamed of for a lifetime, searched for, longed for and never imagined could have, was his very own, and she loved him, too.

Chapter 12/ Sandcastles In The Rain

The rain was beating down in fury, transforming vanilla icing into weak instant coffee, its rhythm competing with the clicking of the orange portable typewriter set up on the ancient oak desk in a corner of the television room, which was mainly Dottie's domain. Watching "My Three Sons" with her grandmother in this room as a young child was a memory she held dear. The room still smelled of Grandma's talcum powder: Yardley's English Lavender. Her spirit had never really left. She wondered what Grandma's reaction to the recent developments would have been, had she lived. She would have been over ninety now. She strained to remember her better, but she had been too young at six to even grasp her loss. The typewriter was a relic from the 1960's and had been a gift to Aunt Audrey from Grandma on some occasion. Now, Dottie was the only one who breathed life into it.

Lights flickered; the night sky lit up and the sound of thunder roared outside the window. Dottie shrieked in terror. Garrett had always called her "Fraidy Cat" and "Crybaby", but thunderstorms were nothing to sneer at, she told herself.

"What is it, honey?"

Marge and Peggy, upon hearing her shriek, materialized by the door.

"That thunder was too close for comfort!"

"Don't you worry none, honey. It can't hurt you."

"We're having crazy weather. We had a snowstorm last week, and now we're getting a thunderstorm. January thaw feels creepy."

"Rain cleanses the earth, baby. All that snow is washin' away."

"Marge, the lights flickered! What if we lose our power?"

"We have candles." she stroked her hair.

"I have two essays to write tonight. They're both due tomorrow. I have Mulhavey for Canadian Lit., and he's a slave driver! He'll give me an F if I'm late one day!"

"You keep workin', honey. Try'n get as much done as you can. I'll bring you some hot chocolate an' cookies."

"What if we lose our power? I can't type by candlelight."

"I can." Peggy volunteered, "It might be kind of fun."

"Thanks, Peggy. You're a doll."

"I'll hang out with you while you work. If the power goes out, I'll step in."

Outside, the thunderstorm raged on.

"I knew I shouldn't have taken this course!" Dottie fumed, hitting the keys with alternating index fingers, "Hilary warned me about Mulhavey."

"Canadian Lit. sounds awfully boring."

"That's the understatement of the century. Canadian writers are so morose, so pompous, and so repressed. They don't like characters who are nice. They make fun of American writers because they write about nice people."

"Why did you take it, then?"

"I needed another English credit for my double major – and I didn't want to be stuck in my senior year taking a whole whack of English courses. This was the only one that didn't conflict with my Sociology courses. So far, I'm maintaining a C-average in it, so I don't want to blow it now."

"As long as you can stick it out, you're okay."

"Mulhavey is so hardened, he has no feelings. He criticizes my essays because I emphasize the emotional aspect of everything I read."

"What's he doing teaching English, then?"

"Because he enjoys torturing people. I figured, as long as I could coast along, and get a passing grade, I would be okay. I'm not looking for B's or anything."

"Looks like the storm is dying down. I'll play some Chicago for you for inspiration."

"I love "If You Leave Me Now". Peter Cetera's so talented!"

Peggy opened the stereo console and turned on the power. The needle automatically landed on the record in place.

"Only five pages left!" Dottie shook out her fingers to relieve pain, "Then, I've got O8's paper to do! I suppose I should start my papers earlier than the night before they're due, but I just can't seem to get around to it."

"Even though Professor O'Hurley is so dashing?" Peggy was smiling affectionately at her.

"I don't like any of my profs. They're all slave drivers. Some, I hate more than others, like Jaycee Manning. She gives all girls a hard time. That lady has problems."

"But O8 is different, right?"

"Okay – I admit, he looks distinguished with his dark-rimmed glasses, his pipe and his red kerchief, like Cary Grant. He smells nice too."

"How do you know? Do you get close enough to sniff him?"

"I try to ask him questions after class as much as I can. But, sometimes it's hard to think of anything to ask."

"You're a smooth operator, Dottie Horncastle. All men better watch out! Whatever happened with that other prof of yours from last year, the one who looked like your all-time paramour, Tony Randall? You were crazy about him."

"He wasn't exactly crazy about me. Any time a prof takes a romantic interest in a student, you can bet she's a slut! They don't waste their time with girls who are not worldly."

“All men are like that.”

“Some say Warren’s like that. They say, if a girl is not worldly, he breaks her heart and walks away...He can’t be with a woman who is not a slut. And, those are the nice people who don’t want to hurt my feelings. Other people are saying he’s a beast.”

“If they’re talking about him so much, they need to find a hobby.”

“People love to talk about this family. They won’t give it a break.”

“They’ll get tired of it eventually.”

“People can be heartless in small towns. They scrutinize your every move. They embellish everything they hear. I never get to see Aunt Edna and Uncle Sid anymore. Mom won’t let them in the house. She made Sydney go away, too.”

“I know you miss them. Honey, it’s okay to talk about them. You don’t have to keep it all in.”

“Mom and Dad would be mad if they knew I was talking about them.”

“They can’t expect you to cut them out of your life forever just because they did.”

“This foolish feud has gone on for long enough. People are saying awful things about Sydney. Around here, failing to conform is a crime worse than murder.”

“She was victimized by everyone. They all turned on her.”

“You know what gets me, Peg? We all had to choose sides and draw battle lines to support Warren without question. He’s the one person who doesn’t seem the least bit disturbed by all the stuff that went down. He lost his job, but he seems happy selling real estate. He still has scores of bimbos hanging all over him. My parents and Uncle Willy are still making him out to be a martyr. I know he’s had losses, but other people lost a lot, too. As much as I love Warren – and I do love him fiercely – I can’t agree with the way he’s been excused for being a naughty boy, and others have been persecuted unfairly. I would gladly give up my life for him, but I can't pledge blind allegiance to him."

Marge was at the door with a tray of steaming mugs and oatmeal cookies.

"Marge, do you ever talk to Aunt Edna?"

"Sure, honey. All the time."

"Are they planning to move to Toronto or anything?"

"I don't think so. At least, she ain't never mentioned it to me."

"There's a big Jewish community there."

"Don't you worry none. They ain't goin' nowhere."

"The way it all played out, you'd think Sydney and Brett were the ones on trial." Peggy said, "Your uncle got off scot free and once again without having to accept responsibility for his actions. He took what he wanted and destroyed it, without a single thought about anyone else. I'm sorry, Dottie, but I can't lie to you. I have a hard time dealing with our perverted justice system. He was rewarded for being a scoundrel."

"I know, but he's my uncle and he's always been good to me. I'm deeply disillusioned by the way he's behaved himself."

"Sydney did the right thing." Peggy said, "You have to stand up for your rights, let people know they can't walk all over you. But she paid a high price for her principles."

"You know, everyone always leaves...First Grandma and Grandpa died...Then Adele...Ella...Jacob moved away...Minette died...Now, Sydney's out of my life."

"She'll be back, Lambkins." Marge held her, "Don't you worry none. Your mama can't stay upset with her own sister too long. Your folks don't spend too much time around here, anyhow. They're always goin' off on trips. Your ma and Miss Mildred stay in Florida for months. Ain't no reason you can't mend fences with Miss Edna while they're away."

"I'm sure they can't forgive me."

"They'd take you back with open arms."

"I don't deserve it. I can't even forgive myself."

"Oh, honey you have to."

"Thank you for caring, guys."

"Anytime, honey. Looks like it's clearin' up. I don't hear no more thunder."

"I'd better get back to work! I still have O8's essay."

"What's O8, darlin'?" Marge asked.

Peggy was laughing wildly.

"When I was typing my prof's name, O'Hurley, on my title page, I forgot to keep pressing the capitals lock button for the apostrophe, so it printed the lower case character: Number eight. His name looked like: O8Hurley. So, Peg and I started calling him O8."

"You girls are a riot." Marge shook her head on her way out.

"One down and one to go." Dottie stapled her pages together.

"Philip Anderson O8Hurley." Peggy sang to the tune of "If You Leave Me Now": "If you fail me now, you'll take away the very soul of me. Ooh, baby, please don't fail me."

"His name was O8. He was a showboat." Dottie sang to the tune of Barry Manilow's "Copacabana": "He wore kerchiefs round his neck and a pipe way out to there...Thought he was so divine...Now he's lost his lungs and he's lost his mind...At the campus...The East Coast campus...where cramming and failing are always in fashion...At the campus...he's lost his mind."

"So will you, if you don't get this done."

Dottie smiled, meticulously feeding a new sheet of blue paper into the typewriter. Everything was as it ought to be. The universe was in harmony. It would, somehow, take care of her. She needed to believe it.

* * *

"Put that thing out." Warren demanded, "You look trashy."

"Isn't that why you love me?" she purred beside him.

"You're going to get cancer, Linda."

"Not me. I plan to defy the odds."

"You can give yourself cancer on your own time. Don't share it with me."

"Well, aren't we testy today?" she put out her cigarette in the red ash tray on the nightstand, "Who rattled your cage?"

"Doesn't this wallpaper give you nightmares?" he studied the psychedelic wallpaper in acid orange, yellow, lime green and magenta.

"I rather like it."

"You would. It matches the orange shag carpet and this funky orange bedspread with the deformed daisies. I get claustrophobic every time I'm in your boudoir."

"Then, take me to yours."

He laughed maniacally.

"You could sneak me in the back door. In a house that big, who'd ever know?"

"Wouldn't that be a hoot, with Jack under the same roof, too!"

"What's he been up to lately?"

"He hasn't been home since before the trial."

206

"Where's he been hiding out?"

"That's what I'd like to know. Sydney hasn't been at her parents' place, either. Don't you find it odd that both our exes have pulled a disappearing act at the same time?" he formed a fist with his left hand, "I'll bet they're off someplace together, fucking the brains out of each other."

"Looks like they outfoxed us. But not for long. I want that bitch dead!"

"She's going through all the men in the family. Mark my words: Tony'll be next. Don and Willy must be waiting their turns with baited breath."

"I want her dead." she threw a heart-shaped pillow across the room, "I want both of them dead. Why don't we do something about it?"

"Because we're not that stupid."

"I'm serious."

"Who do you think they'd be looking at if something were to happen to them?"

"I want them to die. Can't we get someone to knock them off?"

"You'd have to find them first."

"I'll bet Tony knows where they are. Make him tell you."

"My old buddy Sherman can ferret them out, no matter how deep a hole they're hiding in."

"What are you going to do when you find them?"

"You leave that to me."

"Are you going to arrange a fatal accident?"

"You'll have to wait and see."

"Are you just going to torture them with mind games or do some real damage? Disfigure them, cripple them?"

"You're something else, Linda." he shook his head.

"Why, thank you."

"No compliment intended."

"None taken."

"Don't get in my way, Linda. I do things my own way."

"Just remember: If I hadn't called Jack away that night, you wouldn't have been able to get Brett alone. Don't forget that. One word from me and you'll find yourself behind bars."

"If you think you can threaten me, you'd better think again!" his hands closed around her throat, "If you open that pretty little mouth of yours, it'll be the last time you ever do!"

* * *

With snowflakes fluttering around it, the green Victorian bandstand in the town square resembled an enormous snow globe. On the other side of the square, city buses were lined up along the street, extending brotherly hands to cold, weary citizens. Frail, elderly panhandlers stood at the gates of the historic market, playing their guitars and harmonicas, shivering in their threadbare garments. During each trip to the market for fresh fruit and baked goods for the following day's breakfast, she made a point of giving the men enough change for a bowl of hot chicken soup and a coffee next door at Elena's Restaurant. On this day, people scurrying past the men were not stopping to offer them loose change. Behind her, Jack was engaged in a phone conversation with Tony.

"What's wrong?" she asked once he hung up.

"The maintenance guy just up and quit, out of the blue. The next day, this Larry guy showed up looking for work. All his references checked out. Tony hired him, since we were left in the lurch, but he says he has a strange feeling about the guy."

"We should go back. We've had a long, peaceful time away in this beautiful city, at The Grand Hotel, but we have responsibilities back home."

"The snow's supposed to end tonight and the roads should be cleared tomorrow. We can drive back the day after that. Are you sure you're ready?"

"I'm ready."

"I know what's on your mind." he crossed the room to join her by the window and placed an arm around her waist, "It's been on my mind the whole time, too."

"It's unnerving."

"I've been on the phone with Tony during your solo excursions to the market. He's got someone tailing Linda at all times."

"Thank you." she kissed his cheek.

"Your safety is my highest priority."

"Has she been observed engaging in suspicious activities?"

"Not so far. She's got an apartment in an old house on Charlotte Street. And, the only regular visitor she's had is Warren."

"Birds of a feather." she shook her head.

"I'm so sorry my past mistakes have placed you in harm's way. I am not going to let anyone hurt you, Sydney."

"Jack, you have no blame in this. You did not know what she was like."

"I did not choose her. She chose me. All my exes did. I guess it was easier that way, just falling into relationships without any thought or initiative. I took whatever came my way. And it always ended in disaster."

"It's all in the past now. We'll deal with Linda together."

"What did I ever do to deserve you?"

"I could ask the same."

He drew her closer and kissed her hair. The snow outside was turning to rain as the buses pulled away from the bus stop.

Chapter 13/ All Is Fair In Love

"You and I were at this hotel together in 1927 in our past life." she took a sip of her black coffee in the white cup.

"Were we lovers in that life, too?" he reached over to feed her a red grape.

"What do you think?"

"What were our names?"

"Jack and Sydney, of course. How can we be anyone else in any life?"

"Were you this beautiful then, too?" he kissed her bare shoulder.

"Never mind about me. You were devastatingly handsome, just as you are now."

"We must have died young, then." he said wistfully, "1927 is only eleven years before both of us were born in this life. Did we have much time together?"

"Something tells me we found each other at a younger age in that life. We were young, impetuous lovers, rebelling against our families...And, we were so much in love."

"I hope we died together. I'd hate to think one of us died first and the other had to live with the pain of that loss."

"I hope we died together, too. I couldn't bear the thought of living without you now that I've found you, Jack."

"Why did it take us so long to meet in this life, Sydney? We're both forty-one – and we probably didn't even live to be this age in our past life. Why couldn't we have met before this, so we could have had more years together? Why did we have to go through all the bad relationships before we found each other?"

"But we did find each other, Jack. And we have the rest of our lives together."

"I'll bring you breakfast in bed every morning like this." he kissed her, "Fresh fruit and sesame bagels with strawberry cream cheese. But my coffee can't compete with the one from room service."

"Jack, I wish we could move here to John's Bay. It has such a sad and beautiful soul – such a rich history and so much tradition and natural beauty. It grabs at your heart."

"It used to be the cultural center of the province. Ella Fitzgerald and Duke Ellington performed here. Then, it was decided that everything was to be moved to Beavertown, because it's the capital, and that move destroyed any culture the province had. It was a death knell for John's Bay."

"Beavertown is such a soulless town. I despise it. I would love for us to live here in John's Bay and bring my parents here, too. It looks like there's a vibrant Jewish community. They wouldn't feel as alone here. Beavertown is so anti-Semitic."

"At one time, the Jewish community was even more vibrant here. Unfortunately, the younger generation is choosing to leave for places like Toronto and not carrying on the family traditions. They want to be doctors and lawyers and engineers."

"What a shame. No city is complete without family-owned Jewish businesses. The local business district fills me with a warm, homey feeling."

"We can look at our options, honey. Somewhere down the line, we might be able to open up a new jazz club here and live here."

"It's nice to dream."

"Let's make the most of our last day in John's Bay and drive around the city before we head back to Beavertown."

"Jack, will you promise me something?"

"Anything."

"Will you find me in our next life, too?"

"Of course I will. You and I are meant to be reunited in every lifetime for eternity, Sydney."

* * *

Brett and Tony were waiting by the door and ran outside to greet them. Brett squeezed her tight and kissed her cheek. Leading Sydney into the building, she called out to the men engaged in an intense conversation in the parking lot.

"Hey, boys, you can get caught up in here where it's warmer!"

Jack and Tony sauntered in behind them, still whispering, and were met by Chuck, Gene, and Johnny.

"Congratulations, sir." Johnny shook Jack's hand as Gene and Chuck kissed Sydney on the cheek.

"You're my boss now." Brett said to her, "I'd better be on my toes, or you might fire me."

"I've missed you so much, Brett."

"I missed you like crazy. Come on, hon. Let's go downstairs and get ready before we open."

She realized how much she had missed this dressing room. The familiar shabbiness, the mismatched furniture, the musty smell, the tears she and Brett had shed here, and the happiness that had cemented their boundless affection for one another...She could not imagine life away from Brett and their cherished dressing room.

"Don't worry, hon. Tony's guys are keeping an eye on Linda at all times. She can't go to the bathroom without one of them knowing about it."

"I'm causing so much upheaval around here."

"Don't be foolish, hon. After she snuck in here and said: 'You're going to pay for everything you did! You won't know what hit you!', I told Tony to beef up security. I can't let anything happen to you, sweetheart."

"I didn't set out to hurt her. I didn't pursue him. But I do understand why she would see me as a villainess. I've arranged for my parents to stay at The Queen's Hotel for a while until this blows over. Jack and I are still staying there, as well. I don't even know if it's ever going to be safe...I don't know if we'll ever be able to have normal lives again."

"It's all going to be over, sweetheart. There's extra security at the door. Anyone who is not a regular is going to be watched closely." Brett stood behind Sydney, who was seated at the vanity applying her make-up.

"She's just so volatile and unpredictable."

Quickened footsteps and the drone of voices overhead signalled they were now open. Brett felt Sydney shudder under her touch as she held her shoulders firmly.

"You look gorgeous. Come on, let's go upstairs."

There was a congenial crowd of familiar faces. Laughter and cocktails were flowing freely. Jack took her hand and led her backstage. Following the drumroll, Richard announced:

"Ladies and gentlemen, the golden couple, Jack and Sydney Chandler for your listening pleasure!"

Their fans bestowed them with hearty applause.

"Ladies and gentlemen, this beautiful lady has made me the happiest man in the world. She agreed to be my wife and we were married in John's Bay three weeks ago in a private ceremony with only Mr. and Mrs. Goldstein, Brett and Tony present. Now, my wife Sydney and I would like to sing a duet for you: "My One And Only Love".

Brett watched from the Manager's table, tears streaming down her face. Tony placed an arm around her shoulder and smiled knowingly.

* * *

She placed her pocketbook on the dresser and stepped out of her shoes. Sitting at the foot of the bed, she slid her thigh-length stockings down to her ankles to remove them. His eyes transfixed on her bare legs, he attempted to loosen his tie and unbutton his shirt. She crossed the room and whipped off his tie. He unzipped her dress; she wriggled out of it and let it fall. He carried her to the bed.

"Tell me what you want...I'll do anything you want." he nibbled on her ear.

"I want you, Jack...I want to smell you, taste you, touch your skin; I want to see your eyes and hear you when you come. I love you."

Jack's lovemaking soothed every fear. Serenity washed over her. He was a considerate lover, focused only on her pleasure, delaying his own fulfillment. He was responsive and sensitive. She wanted everything to remain this way forever.

*　*　*

"Miss Audrey's on the warpath. Stay clear of her, darlin'." Marge warned Peggy.

"I reckon she's not too pleased for the happy couple." Peggy said.

"The rest of them ain't too happy, either. They're actin' like they're in mournin'."

"Would they rather see him with that looney tunes Linda? I can't believe these people."

"If it weren't for my little lamb, Miss Dottie, I would've left this job by now. Your Pops got the right idea, retirin' next year."

"I agree. You should, too, Mom. They're making too many demands. It's affecting your health. We can get an apartment for the three of us. I make good money. You could work as a seamstress. Pops is going to be getting his Old Age Pension by next year anyway. We can get out of this madhouse."

"What about Miss Dottie?"

215

"It would do her good to get out of this place, too. I was thinking she could get an apartment close to us, so we could spend even more time together."

"I don't like the way these folks been treatin' Miss Sydney at all."

"Neither do I."

This was Dottie. Standing in the doorway in her pink mohair sweater and her jeans, with her hair down, she spoke solemnly.

"You look so pretty, darlin'." Marge said.

"Thank you. I have a date. That is, if this one actually shows up."

"He'd be a darn fool not to."

"I miss Sydney." she joined them at the kitchen table, "I'd give anything to be friends with her again."

"Then, you should tell her, sweetie." Peggy said.

"She must hate me."

"No, she doesn't."

"If I were her, I'd hate me."

"Go and talk to her."

"I don't even know where she and Jack are living now."

"Go to the club. You're legal now."

"Peg, that's a great idea!"

"Take your date there, honey." Marge suggested.

"He'd be really mad if I took him to a classy place like that, Marge. Guys my age don't like anything nice. Clara says I've got to give up on my unrequited crushes on older men and go for boys my age. I'm forcing myself to, but it's really hard."

"I hope tonight goes well for you, honeybunch."

"Thanks. I'm keeping my expectations low, so I can't be disappointed or hurt."

"Oh, honey…"

"It's okay, Marge. I know I'm not what boys my age are looking for. It's going to be a short date, anyway – that is, if he shows up. We're supposed to get a storm tonight and I want to get home before it gets bad."

"Who is this lucky fellow? What's his name?"

"Ian. Ian Fisher. He's in some of my classes and knows some of the people I know. I'm surprised he asked me out at all. We barely know each other."

"I hope it works out for you, honey."

"I want to get home before that storm. They predicted 20 cm. I don't want to be stuck in it…Hey, Peg, do you remember that big storm we had a couple of years ago? We were only supposed to get 20 cm., but we ended up getting something like 50! The whole city shut down. Even the buses were off the roads."

"I remember that one well. I was stranded at work. I had to stay late on my own to finish up some 'urgent' stuff. By the time I was done, there was 10 ft. of snow outside. I couldn't get a cab, and no buses were running. Luckily, the lady who worked upstairs for the insurance company gave me a ride when her husband came to pick her up in his big truck. God was looking out for me."

"I remember we were just changing over to metric then. The radio announcer said we were going to get 20 kilometers of snow!"

"He was right. We did!" Peggy laughed.

"I guess I'd better get my coat and stuff." Dottie rose, "I don't want him to think I'm some snooty rich girl who keeps her dates waiting."

"He's the one who should be trying to make a good impression." Peggy reminded her.

“Nobody cares about what impression they make on me, Peg.” she started toward the front entrance, “I don't matter that much to anyone.”

Chapter 14/ The Darkest Night

"Hey, Dory, let's go to your cousin's swanky club."

Dottie eyed the young boy with suspicion. They had only been out on five movie dates, and now he was feigning interest in something she cared about. It could only mean one thing: He wanted to amp up the pressure to make her put out. Not that it was going to work. But he didn't need to know that just yet.

"Sure." she smiled politely.

They were at the traffic light half a block away from the club. He had started calling her Dory lately, at first only when he introduced her to his friends, but now, all the time. He parked his rusty Falcon in the parking lot. She noticed for the first time that evening that he had not worn jeans, which meant coming here was a premeditated move, not a spur of the moment decision. What would he have done had she worn jeans instead of dress pants? Told her to change before they left her house?

Johnny greeted them at the door.

"Hello, Miss Horncastle. Nice to have you back."

"Thanks, Johnny."

As they were shown to their table, Ian's eyes surveyed their surroundings, his mouth gaping open.

"Who did you come here with before?" he wanted to know.

"My best friend Peggy."

"What year is she in? Does she have any classes with us?"

"She's not in school. She works as a legal assistant."

"Oh. Okay."

A waiter arrived to take their order.

"A Tom Collins." Ian said, with an air of self-importance.

"A Pink Lady, please." she said.

"Hey, man, what're you doing here?"

She heard a vaguely familiar voice behind them.

"Hey, man, what's shaking?" Ian responded, as an equally gangly figure came around the side and stood next to him.

Dottie's heart sank. Of all the people in town, he had to be there. Ben from high school. Except, he wanted to be called by his full name now: Bentley.

"What're you doing later?" Ben asked Ian.

"Chilling with my chick."

"Wanna go to Steve's party?"

"Sure."

"He's got premium grade dope." he snickered.

"Cool, man."

"Charlene and I are going to the Silverwood Motel after." he smirked.

"Us, too." Ian said.

Dottie froze to her seat. She scrambled to make her way to the Manager's table.

"Hi, Tony." she tapped him on the shoulder.

"Dottie! What are you doing here?" he turned around.

"Bringing me here was my date's idea of melting my resistance. He's friends with this creepy guy from my high school. I got weird vibes from them, so I ditched him. I think they're up to something."

"Don't worry. You can stay here with me."

"Thanks, Tony."

Brett was concluding her set with "Moonlight In Vermont". Dottie positioned herself behind a woman with a bouffant hairstyle at a nearby table, in order to block Ian and Ben's view of herself. Brett joined them at the table and embraced her.

"What a nice surprise, Dottie!"

"She's hiding from her date and his friend." Tony explained.

"You just stick with me, sweetheart. I'll protect you." Brett patted her knee.

"Jack and Sydney are going on together next." Tony said.

"I'm so glad you and Sydney made up, sweetheart." Brett said, "You know, she loves you so much."

"I love her, too. I cried all the time when we weren't on speaking terms. I never wanted things to be that way. I never wanted her to be hurt."

"I know, hon. Sydney understood."

All eyes were averted to the stage following the drumroll. They began the set with "Our Love Is Here To Stay". Halfway through the song, all the lights flickered. Ahhs were heard from the audience. Staff members headed toward the back stairs to the basement.

"What's going on?" Dottie asked Tony.

"Some sort of an electrical issue. I'll go down and check the panel."

"Be careful, hon." Brett said.

In a matter of seconds, Tony returned, his face beet-red. Jack and Sydney vacated the stage and Richard took the microphone to announce an evacuation. Tony whispered to Brett:

"There's smoke in the basement. I couldn't even get down the stairs. The fire department's on their way. Take my car keys." he handed them to her, "Take Dottie home and stay with her until I get there."

The bone-chilling sound of the fire alarm deafened everyone. Brett took Dottie by the arm and swiftly led her outside. Dazed patrons scurried like beetles as sprinklers rained down on them. Smoke was filling the main level. An explosion set the entire lounge ablaze. Tony ordered the remaining reluctant staff members, Johnny, Chuck and Gene to leave, however they refused.

"Jack! Sydney! Has anybody seen them?" Tony called out, "I think they're still in the building!"

"Boss, they're over here!" Johnny opened the curtains to the backstage area where two mounds were buried under rubble and one lay under a fallen beam.

The men lifted the beam and dug out the two unconscious victims. Tony and Gene carried Jack as Johnny and Chuck carried Sydney outside as fire trucks drove into the fire lane with sirens blaring.

* * *

"It's been two hours. Where's Tony?" Dottie sobbed, "Where are Sydney and Jack?"

"When I heard them sirens so close, I had an uneasy feelin'." Marge replenished the supply of chocolate chip cookies on the kitchen table, "Then, when you two showed up lookin' like little stray kittens, I knew it was really bad."

"I hope they're all okay." Brett said.

"I can get Shawn to fix you a stronger drink, Miss Morrow." Peggy offered.

"No thanks, dear." Brett said, "I need my wits about me. Besides, I might need to drive. And, call me Brett. No need for formalities."

When the telephone rang, all four of them bolted. Peggy answered it.

"Yes sir, Mr. Tony." she handed the phone to Brett.

"Sweetheart, what's happening? We've been worried sick...No! No!"

"Brett, what's going on?" Dottie was hanging on her arm, "Tell us!"

"I will. Be careful, hon. Love you. Bye." she hung up, "Sydney and Jack are in Intensive Care. That's where he was calling from. It doesn't look good. We have to wake up the family and get over there."

"I'll get Aunt Edna and Uncle Sid. I have a key to their house." Dottie said.

"I'll call Ryan and tell him to bring their car around." Peggy said, "And I'll knock on all the doors to wake up the family."

"I'll get Shawn to be on alert here, 'cause I'm comin' with you, too." Marge said.

"I think I should go with Aunt Edna and Uncle Sid in their car, Brett." Dottie said.

"Of course, sweetheart. I'll take Marge and Peggy with me."

They arrived at the hospital parking lot in a caravan of four cars and rushed into the building. They were glued together in the two tight elevators. Tony met them on the seventh floor.

"No one can see them yet. The next twenty-four hours are critical. All we can do now is pray."

Mildred and Annette were holding up the pale Audrey by her arms.

"My son...My Jack...I have to be with him."

"No dear, we're not allowed to see him yet." Mildred said.

"Sydney's condition is worse." Tony told Brett, Marge and Peggy, "Johnny found them backstage. It looks like they were trying to make it to the side exit, but the flames were so intense, they fell back. Sydney was trying to shield Jack by stepping between him and a falling beam. From the positions we found them in, that is how it appeared. She has a nasty head wound.

Both of them inhaled a lot of smoke. Jack has cuts on his face where some ceiling tiles fell on him.”

Peggy and Marge attempted to comfort a sobbing Brett by taking turns hugging her. Donald and Willard stood stoically. Dottie knelt down and placed her arms around the weeping Edna and Sid. Warren approached Tony with a furrowed brow.

“Tone – can you tell me the name of that new maintenance guy you hired?”

“How do you know about that?”

“Richard and I frequent the same watering holes. He keeps me up to date. He mentioned this new guy. Apparently, there was something you didn’t like about him. Can you tell me his name and address?”

“Larry Matthews. He lives in that old apartment building at the corner of George and York Streets. Do you think this was arson?”

“Let me check it out.” he touched his arm reassuringly.

“It’s that woman!” Audrey was shouting, “She’s been nothing but trouble since the day she came here! She’s cursed our family!”

“You’d better watch your mouth, Toots!” Brett lunged at her, “If it weren’t for her, your son would be dead now! She saved his life. She placed her own life in jeopardy to save his. You have some gall! If he hadn’t met her, he would’ve married that psychopath Linda! How would you like having a psycho like that instead for a daughter-in-law? Linda’s the one who torched the club in the first place! I’d bet money on it!”

“Ladies, that’s enough.” Donald took two steps forward.

“Tell your lunatic sister to shut her filthy mouth, or I’ll do it for her!” Brett shook her fist.

“Somebody please help!” Dottie was screaming, ”I think Uncle Sid is having a heart attack!”

Ryan bolted immediately and returned with medical staff, who wheeled him down the hall. Edna and Dottie followed behind, holding on to one another. Marge caught up with them.

Warren was at the payphone, speaking in a hushed tone.

"Hal – listen. Track down Larry Matthews. He lives in that old monstrosity on the corner of George and York. Deal with him. You know what to do. I'll be in touch later."

Annette and Mildred were huddled together glaring at Brett across the room.

"What do you think you're looking at? You biddies have no conscience! That angel saved your precious Jack's life and you're probably sitting there, wishing her dead. I hope God strikes all of you snobs dead!"

"Brett, honey, let's sit down." Tony led her to an orange vinyl seat, "Everyone's nerves are on edge."

"They've hated her since day one! She's worth ten of you!" she turned to the women again.

"It's all right, Brett." Tony held her, "Sydney's going to be all right."

"I'm with Brett on this one." Warren stated, "You've always despised her and you're probably wishing her dead right now. She's never done anything to you. Why don't you grow up and start acting like adults?"

A speechless Brett looked at him in astonishment. Warren winked at her.

"I have to step out for a while." he said, "Can you ladies try to behave yourselves? Audrey? Millie? Annie? I'm leaving Tony in charge to keep you in line."

"Times like this bring out a side of people no one knew existed." Peggy said, taking a seat on the other side of Brett and rubbing her back.

"Take a look at yourselves!" Warren shouted, "There's a man having a heart attack because his daughter is fighting for her life and all that you old biddies can do is say malicious things about an innocent woman." He stormed out.

"He is right." Donald said, "We have to try to refrain from expressing negative remarks which might offend others."

A silence fell upon the somber group. All averted their eyes to the terrazzo floor.

* * *

Warren slammed the door behind him.

"You crazy bitch! What did you do?"

Linda winked coquettishly at him with her crooked smile.

"What did you do, dammit?" his fingers dug into her forearms as he shook her.

"You're hurting me!" she attempted to free herself, "Let go of me, you brute!"

"This is nothing." he tightened his hold, dragged her to the sofa and threw her down, "You're going to be feeling a lot more pain."

"What's come over you all of a sudden? Have you gone nuts?"

"What did you do, Linda?" he roared, "What the hell were you thinking?"

"I thought you'd be pleased. It went down exactly the way we both wanted."

"You fucking psycho!" he pulled her up by the hair and slammed her head against the wall.

"They both got what they deserved. Larry's on his way to the hospital right now to finish her off."

"Wrong!" his fist came down on her face, "Larry's on his way to the morgue – just like you're going to be very soon! I'm way ahead of you, bitch!"

"Let me go! I'll scream!"

"Just try. I'll rip out your vocal cords." he slapped her across the face.

He threw her down on the wood floor and knelt over her, pinning her arms with his knees. His hands tightened around her throat. He continued to squeeze until her body was limp and she was looking up at him with the bulging eyes of a frog. He carried her to the bedroom and propped her up in bed, posing her like a mannequin. He lit a cigarette and placed it between her fingers. Searching the room frantically, he spotted the acetone in the slender pink plastic bottle labeled "Cutex". He doused her with its contents, and threw a match on her before slipping out the door and down the stairs, the sweet smell of acetone trailing behind him.

*   *   *

Tony and Johnny selected a table by the window in the musty coffee shop with well-worn wood tables.

"Both the police and the fire department have concluded their investigations." Tony spoke solemnly, "They found two bodies in the bar area, Johnny. Burnt beyond recognition. They need dental records to identify them. This is an absolute horror. I phoned every single staff member to make sure they were all accounted for."

"One good thing, sir: The Castle was closed for renos, so there was nobody there. I don't know how both businesses could've been evacuated without more fatalities. It went up so quick."

"You're right, Johnny. It could've been far worse."

An older man with a green apron came to take their order.

"Two black coffees." Tony said.

"Did they rule it as arson, sir?" Johnny asked once they were alone.

"They claim it was accidental."

"But it went up so fast, boss. It was an inferno. Electrical fires are intense, but this was something else."

"They found no evidence of an accelerant. They said aluminum wiring was the reason for the way it happened. It's a major fire hazard and there has been a sharp increase in electrical fires since they started using it. Overloading circuits results in overheating and fires, instead of tripping breakers as in copper wiring. Aluminum wiring was banned five years ago. Willow Place was built in 1972, the heyday of aluminum wiring."

"But, boss, we haven't had any trouble for eight years."

"Sometimes it can take years of regular use to weaken it before it causes fires. The more it ages, the more dangerous it becomes. When they first realized this and banned it, why didn't they order all aluminum wiring to be removed from existing homes and businesses? It's not enough to just stop using it. Let's see what the insurance company's investigators say. I'm not buying that it was accidental. We've always been very careful."

"I think you're right, boss. That new maintenance guy might've deliberately overloaded the circuits."

"He was probably working for that crazy woman Jack was engaged to. She was always coming around making all sorts of threats. Total nutcase. I hope they lock her up and throw away the key."

"Boss, do you think there's any connection between this and the fire on Charlotte Street later that night where a woman was smoking in bed? They still haven't released her identity."

"I don't know what to think, Johnny. I told the police about my suspicions. They haven't been able to track down Larry Matthews. He must've skipped town. I also gave them Linda's name, but I don't know where she lives now."

The man with the apron served their coffee in white porcelain cups.

"Are you going to rebuild, sir?"

"It's all on hold until Jack and Sydney recover and we come to a mutual decision. I think they'd want to rebuild."

"That would be nice, sir. I was worried you'd sell the land and someone would build a sleazy bar, pool hall or disco."

"Ironically, Brett had suggested I change the name of the restaurant from "The Castle" to "Anthony's", and Jack had mentioned he wanted "Chandler's Lounge" changed to "Sydney's Place". Maybe we'll make those changes after rebuilding."

"I hope they both recover quickly, sir."

"Me, too. They are the life and soul of that place. I feel lost dealing with all of this on my own."

"You're not alone, sir. We're all here for you."

"Thanks, Johnny."

They drank their coffee in silence watching the traffic on a slushy, grey Queen Street.

*   *   *

Audrey knocked on the heavy wooden door.

"Come in." a gruff male voice answered.

"Willard," she closed the door behind her, "I need your help."

"Have a seat, Audrey."

Behind the enormous antique cherry desk, Willard appeared shrunken and shriveled.

"I have to protect Jack and the family from that gold-digger." Audrey sat across from him, "Thankfully, Jack hasn't had the opportunity to draw up a new will, so I'm still his beneficiary."

"I think I see where you're going with this."

"I need all your contacts. You'll have to call in favors from your Freemason pals, doctors, administrators, the coroner, and such. I'll also need your guys for new identities, transportation and a few other details."

"That's a tall order, Audrey. But, don't worry. Everything you need will be at your disposal."

"Thank you, Willard." Audrey inhaled deeply.

* * *

"Sydney, please, please come back to us, my baby." Edna wept, cautiously caressing her unconscious daughter's arm, "Sweetheart, your dad and I love you and need you so very much. Please open your eyes."

Warren observed silently through the glass, his head bowed, and wiped his tears before returning to the waiting area where Brett and Peggy were seated on each side of Dottie.

"She's going to get better, isn't she?"

"Of course she is."

"I'm just so relieved Uncle Sid's getting better now."

"That poor man. It's so unfair." Brett said, "You know, I think I'll ask Tony to post a guard outside Sydney's room. I don't trust that Audrey woman. She's up to something."

"I have to go to work now, but I'll be back later." Peggy rose, "I have to catch a bus home, get showered and freshened up first."

"Ryan can drive you, hon. He's with the Goldsteins now." Brett suggested.

"Brett," Peggy said, "There's already a guard outside Miss Sydney's room this morning. I saw him earlier when I went to the ladies' room."

"Tony must've already thought of it."

"I'll get Ryan." Dottie volunteered.

"I can take you home, Peggy." Warren spoke up from across the room.

"Please don't go to any trouble, sir."

"No trouble. I'm going home, anyway."

"Thank you, sir. I'll be back after work, Dottie." Peggy waved at Dottie and Brett.

"I hope you don't mind if I sit with Uncle Sid for a while, Brett." Dottie said, "Aunt Edna's still with Sydney."

"Please go ahead, dear. Tony'll be here soon, anyway."

When Tony came off the elevator, Brett went up to kiss him on the cheek.

"How're you holding up?" she asked him.

"As well as can be expected. How about you? Do you want me to take you home so you can sleep?"

"No, hon. I can't leave Sydney. By the way, thanks for posting the guard outside her room."

"Guard? What guard?"

"If you didn't post him, who did?"

"Beats me."

"I feel better knowing he's there. No offense, hon, but I don't trust your family."

"Neither do I."

"Edna's with her now. When she comes out, I'd like to go in."

"You slept in a chair by her bed all night, didn't you?"

"I don't want to be away from her for one second."

"I know. Let's sit here for a few minutes. I want to fill you in on the latest developments."

"Did they identify those bodies?"

"Yes. They were Dottie's date and his friend."

"What were they doing behind the bar?"

"Trying to steal some booze, to take advantage of the commotion."

"Have the police found Larry Matthews yet?"

"Yes."

"Where was he?"

"At the morgue. He was the John Doe they found in a back alley, assumed to be a homeless man. There's more: The woman who died in the Charlotte Street fire the same night as the club fire, turned out to be Linda. Her name isn't released yet because when her parents came to identify her body, they insisted on an autopsy. The results were not what anyone expected. She did not die in an accidental fire caused by smoking in bed. Her lungs were clear, which means she was dead before the fire started. They also found an accelerant, so it's ruled as a homicide and arson."

"Instead of answers, there are more questions."

"The new investigation revealed the circuits at the club were overloaded beyond normal human error. Listen, honey, you need to eat something."

"Why don't we go down to the cafeteria for a quick coffee and Danish so we can come back up quickly?"

He led her to the elevators with an arm around her shoulder.

* * *

"You'll have to wait, Ma'am. Mr. Horncastle is in there now. They only allow one visitor at a time."

She caught a glimpse of Warren through the window.

"Why did you allow Warren Horncastle in there?" she asked the guard.

"But, Ma'am, Mr. Horncastle is the one who hired me."

"In that case, I'll come back later." she returned to the waiting room.

"Warren's in there with her." she told Tony.

"Warren?"

"It turns out he's the one who hired the guard."

"That's interesting."

"He must know something."

"He must think she's in danger."

"He's trying to protect her. I believe he's sincere."

"So do I."

"I'm so worried about her, Tony. She has so much internal damage. I'm terrified they're going to claim she's brain-dead and ask Edna and Sid to disconnect her life support. My Sydney is a fighter. She's trying to come back to us."

*　*　*

"Find a homeless man with Jack's build and coloring...That's your job! Offer him money, promise him work, do whatever you need to do to get him here. Clean him up, dress him up in clean clothes, and bring him up the stairs. Don't use the elevator."

She lowered her voice when Warren entered her field of vision.

"What are you up to now, Sis? Plotting and scheming as usual? Who's your latest victim?" he smirked.

"You're the only schemer in this family. Stop eavesdropping on innocent conversations and stirring things up."

"As you wish, dear sister." he sauntered to the waiting room where he found Tony and Brett.

233

"Watch Audrey closely. She's up to something." he said.

"She does seem to be acting in a peculiar way. I'll keep a close eye on her." Tony said.

"She's never approved of their marriage. There's no telling what she's capable of. I've instructed the guards to keep her out of Sydney's room, no matter what." Brett said.

"She wouldn't get her own hands dirty. She'd get someone to do what she instructs." Warren shook his head in exasperation.

"Her guys might be clever enough to con the guards. That's why it's imperative that one of us be in there with her around the clock." Brett said.

"I agree." Warren sat beside Tony, "I think that was Audrey's original plan to get someone to disconnect her from her life support. That's why I hired the guards. Now, she's cooking up a new diabolical scheme. I heard her on the phone telling someone to find a homeless man with Jack's build and coloring, to promise him money, and to bring him here. I don't like the sound of it one bit. I'm going to stay on her like a bad rash."

"She's denying all of us access to Jack." Tony said, "Even Dottie is not allowed to see him. Those thugs she's hired to guard his room look like convicted felons."

"The only time she leaves his side is to use the payphone." Brett said.

"I'm going to blow her right out of the water when I find out what's going on." Warren stated.

"Let's all keep one another posted on her activities." Brett suggested, "It's up to us to look out for Sydney."

"You've got a deal." Warren rose, "I'm going back to her room."

Small and vulnerable, connected to a myriad of machines, she was oblivious to the goings on around her.

"Sydney, please wake up." he held her hand, "Open your beautiful eyes for me."

The urgent beeping of the cardiac monitor alerted him that she was flatlining.

"Nurse! Nurse!" he ran outside, "Somebody please help!"

The staff arrived promptly with a crash cart.

"Sir, you'll have to wait outside."

As though in a dream, he observed them working on her.

"Clear!" the doctor shouted.

"We're losing her!" he heard one of the nurses calling out frantically.

"Again!" the doctor commanded.

"We're losing her!"

"Don't give up now, Stormy! You can't give up now! You've got to hang in there!" tears were streaming down his face.

Behind him, Edna and Sid appeared – then, Dottie, Brett and Tony, followed by Peggy and Marge. A heavy silence surrounded them. From the corner of his eye, Warren observed Edna falling to the floor and managed to catch her. They heard the cardiac monitor resume its regular rhythm and sighed in relief. Nurses appeared at Edna's side and led her away. Warren held a sobbing Dottie in his arms and let his own tears fall on her hair.

Chapter 15/ The End Of The Road

Marin sat beside Brett in the waiting room with the putrid orange vinyl chairs.

"We almost lost her, baby. It was touch and go. When Edna heard them saying 'We're losing her!', she fainted dead away and had to be admitted herself. We're going out of our minds with worry. They were able to save her, but Sydney still hasn't regained consciousness. I'm terrified they're going to claim she's braindead, so they can harvest her organs. They do that in all hospitals, you know. And ninety-nine times out of a hundred, the patients are not braindead at all. I told Edna and Sid not to consent to disconnecting her life support, no matter how much the doctors try to persuade them. Sydney's going to come back to us; I know it."

"Mom, please try to get some rest. I don't want you to get sick, too." Marin kissed her cheek, "I wish I could've been here earlier, but I didn't want to give you my bad flu."

"It's okay, sweetheart. You're here now."

"Why don't you put your head on my shoulder and try to catch a few winks?" she propped her up beside her and placed Brett's head on her shoulder.

"Thank you, sweetheart." Brett closed her eyes.

Tony and Dottie were coming off the elevator and approaching them, unnoticed by Marin who was whispering a lullaby into Brett's ear.

"She finally dozed off." she spoke in a low voice when Dottie tapped her on the shoulder.

"This must be a busy spot tonight." Dottie said softly, "When Tony and I first came in, on our way to the elevators, we saw a couple of orderlies coming off the freight elevator with a gurney. The patient had his face covered with bandages, like Jack, and he was hooked up to an I.V. and stuff. They sure were in a big hurry to get him into the waiting ambulance. They must be airlifting him to Halifax or something."

"I hope they don't have to do that with Sydney or Jack." Marin said, "Mom couldn't cope with that."

"No one's said anything about it, so I hope things are okay with the way they are, at least for now."

"CODE BLUE! Room 74! CODE BLUE! Room 74!" was announced and staff scurried down the hall with the crash cart.

"It's Jack!" Dottie bolted, and ran after them, with Tony in pursuit.

"Sydney! Is it Sydney again?" Brett was jolted awake.

"It's Jack." Marin said solemnly.

"No!" Brett took her hand and pulled her in the direction of the room.

Through the window, they could see the staff attempting to revive him with repeated shocks. They documented the time of death as 7:12 p.m. In the hallway, Dottie and Brett collapsed on the floor, holding each other. Annette and Mildred hugged. Audrey was wailing like a wounded poodle in Willard's arms. Tony held Marin. Warren's icy glare was fixed on Audrey. She shot back a threatening glance in his direction. His unrelenting gaze averted her eyes and she broke free from Willard, turning her back to Warren.

* * *

"What did we do to you, Stormy?" Warren sat on the chair beside Sydney's bed, "We made a sacrificial lamb out of you."

The monitor continued beeping its reassuring rhythm as she lay ashen and frail before him.

"My family treated you worse than dirt. None of them gave you a chance or tried to know the real you. I was no better. But I swear I'll make it up to you, somehow. Please wake up, Stormy. You've got to wake up. You can't leave us now."

Her eyes opened slowly, unable to focus.

"Jack..." she murmured, "Jack..."

"You're back!" he grasped both of her hands.

"Warren? Where's Jack?" she glanced around her groggily, "Why am I here?"

"You were in a fire."

"Are my parents okay?"

"They're fine. The fire was at Chandler's."

"Is Jack all right? Can I see him?"

"Sydney, Jack...He was also injured."

"Warren, what are you keeping from me?"

"Sydney...Listen to me closely. It's probably best you hear it from me first. People are going to tell you that Jack is gone. Please don't believe them. I'm convinced there's some sort of deception going on and my sister's hiding him somewhere. I'm going to leave no stone unturned until I bring him back to you."

"I don't understand."

"Don't give up hope."

"What's going on, Warren?"

"You just concentrate on getting stronger, Sydney. Remember: Jack is missing, but alive. I intend to prove that. Don't let anyone convince you otherwise. Just play along with them."

"How did the fire start?"

"It was arson. The people who were responsible for it are both dead now."

"I'm very confused about this."

"It's okay. You don't need to think about any of that now. I need to let the staff know you're awake, so they can check your vitals. Your parents and Brett are going to want to see you right away. You and I will have a chance to talk about this soon." he squeezed her hand.

"Thank you, Warren."

* * *

"We'll all keep our eyes open and report to each other if we hear about or notice something that might be a clue." Dottie said, as the group huddled around a table in the back of The Admiral.

"No funeral...No burial...A rushed cremation...Then, she leaves town without notice for destinations unknown, takes the urn with her...I think Willy's in on it. There's no way she could pull off something of this enormity without some help from very high and very low places." Warren said.

"Who is the poor guy they substituted for him?" Brett shuddered, "If Jack is indeed alive, then a gruesome murder was committed to fake his death."

"A gruesome murder no one will ever be held accountable for." Tony shook his head.

"I have detectives working on it. Those who are responsible for that murder are going to be brought to justice. We owe it to Sydney and to Jack." Warren said.

"We need to rebuild Chandler's into a place that will make them both proud." Brett told Tony, "I hope Sydney wants to go ahead with that plan."

"Sydney definitely wants to rebuild, but insists her name be kept out of it. She wants the lounge renamed "Jack's Place". I'm changing "The Castle" to "Anthony's", and "Willow Place" is now going to be "Chandler Palace", which Sydney and I decided on together. A brand new building with proper wiring. Sydney suggested "Streamline Moderne" style in white stucco, with rounded walls, glass bricks, and portholes for a true vintage look.

It was Jack's favorite style of architecture, but in the 1960's and 70's, builders were not skilled in creating aesthetically pleasing structures. All they could produce were ugly boxes with bad wiring and tacky interiors."

"When Jack comes back, he'll be deeply touched by the way you and Sydney have done things according to his taste and wishes." Brett placed his hand over his.

* * *

Jack gone...She begrudged the sun for rising each day without a care, the stars for shining with such brazen abandon, spring for its timid attempts at settling down, and life itself for going on without Jack. She begrudged herself the ability to awaken each morning to the emptiness of being alive.

Brett stood in the doorway and knocked softly on the door frame.

"Brett!" she beamed.

"Hi, sweetheart. Diane called me and said she wants to meet with both of us here in your room in an hour."

"I had forgotten about our lawsuit, with all the other stuff going on. So many things have changed since then, Brett. I don't feel right about it anymore."

"Neither do I. I wonder if it's too late to withdraw."

"Warren has bent over backwards, trying to be helpful. I can't betray him like that."

"Seeing you in here had a powerful impact on him, sweetheart. I believe he sincerely cares about you."

"He's been so attentive and kind. I don't feel comfortable having a private room when there are people in wards, but I didn't want to hurt his feelings, so I went along with it."

"He's pulled out all the stops to prove Jack is alive, and he is not going to give up until he brings him back to you."

"Does he really believe Jack could be alive?"

"Too many things don't add up."

"Hello, ladies." Diane was at the door in her grey tweed suit.

"Diane, it's good to see you."

"How are you feeling now, Sydney?" she shook her hand.

"Much better, thank you."

"I wanted to meet with both of you today, because we have a very generous offer on the table. Warren Horncastle went against the advice of his own attorney to settle out of court with an unusually high offer."

"Brett and I were talking before you arrived." Sydney said, "In light of the recent events, we feel it would be inappropriate for us to benefit financially."

"These recent events are the reason he wants to set things right, I believe."

"He's gone above and beyond already." Sydney said, "I can't take advantage of him."

"I feel the same way." Brett joined, "He's a changed man. In his own way, he sincerely cares about Sydney. This whole lawsuit business…It was never about the money, anyway."

"I'm sorry we wasted your time, Diane. Just send me your bill for your services."

"All your legal expenses have been paid – both of you."

"We've been a complete waste of your time, Diane." Brett said.

"Not at all. The publicity surrounding the criminal trial has raised awareness. As a result, more women will have the courage to come forward and report being raped by their sexual partners. I don't anticipate too many cases concluding as amicably as yours, though." Diane rose, "Listen, it's been a pleasure working with you ladies. I'm glad things worked out on their own. I wish both of you the best."

"Thank you, Diane, for everything." Sydney rose from her bed to see her to the door.

* * *

"You didn't accept my offer." Warren sat at the foot of her bed.

"Both Brett and I felt it was water under the bridge. So much has happened since then. None of us are the same people we were then."

"I wanted you to know that I'm sorry, Stormy. I'm sorry I treated you the way I did. You never deserved any of that."

"I'm sorry, too."

"You have no reason to be."

"You and I – We were meant to be friends, not lovers."

"That would never have worked, Stormy."

"Why?"

"Because I would've never given up trying to get you in the sack."

"You know, all you had to do was ask me what you wanted to know."

"That's not the real reason I pursued you." he stroked her cheek, "I wanted you the moment I laid my eyes on you. It wouldn't have made any difference who you were, what your circumstances were; I had to have you."

"Lust at first sight." she smiled, "For both of us."

"So cynical. You don't believe in love at first sight?"

"There's no such thing. People mistake lust for love, but love needs to develop over time and grow as two people discover each other's inner beauty, as well as flaws and shortcomings. Love is respecting the other person, accepting the whole package...not just about animal attraction. Love can't happen in a fleeting moment. Lust and obsession, yes, but not love. And, if that initial attraction deepens into love over time, those two people are blessed. Love is very rare; lust is commonplace.”

“We definitely had lust at first sight, Stormy. But, in time, I realized there was something different about you. I saw the storm in your eyes. I knew there was so much more to you than anyone else I’d ever known before.”

“I don’t know what to say.”

“You weren’t just another roll in the hay. You were always special. When I saw you lying here, fighting for your life, I finally had to admit it to myself. I couldn’t run from it anymore. I love you, Stormy. I’ve always been in love with you.”

“I care about you, too, Warren. As a friend.”

“I can handle being friends.” he smiled wistfully.

“Thank you.”

“I know Jack is your one true love, and he’s going to come back to you.”

“I don’t want to get my hopes up. If he is alive and out there somewhere, I have to ask myself: Did he leave on his own accord, or was he coerced? And what was the motivation behind each scenario?”

“I hope all those questions can be answered for you, Stormy. I’m going to get to the bottom of it.”

“I appreciate that, Warren.”

“What are your long-term plans, or have you had the chance to think about that yet?”

“I’m going to leave Beavertown. Uncle Ira and Aunt Ethel have offered me a job at their antique shop and their lovely carriage house as lodging. How can I turn that down?”

“What about “Chandler Palace”?”

"Tony'll keep me up to date, and I'll come down from time to time. But I just think everyone needs some space from me. I've caused too much upheaval and controversy here."

"You're definitely a force to be reckoned with, Sydney Chandler, and you've changed every life you've touched, but no one would want to see you leave. You're going to be missed."

"Thank you."

"I hope the change of scenery'll do you good."

"I appreciate everything you've done, Warren, and I'm happy to see you and Brett getting along, too."

"See? You're a good influence on me. I'm a better man for knowing you."

"That better man was always inside you, Warren, waiting for you to unlock his prison cell and grant his freedom."

* * *

"That mystery patient's coming around now." a young nurse with a blonde ponytail said, "He keeps repeating something...Someone's name...Sounds like Cindy."

"Must be his girlfriend's name." an older nurse remarked.

"Or wife's? What is he doing here, in Boston, anyway? Don't they have hospitals in Canada?"

"He wanted to come here just to meet you, Natasha."

"Whatever the reason is for him being here, I'm not planning to let him get away from me, now that I've found him." the younger nurse said.

"How do you know you'll like him when you get to know him? He might be a wife-beater or something."

"No, I don't think so. You can tell he's a sweet, gentle guy. Whoever this Cindy is, she doesn't stand a chance now. She'll be history soon."

"You sure don't waste any time, Tash. Better watch out for that Mama Bear. She looks tough."

"She doesn't scare me, Jess."

"Something's been nagging at me since they brought him here. He looks so familiar, but I can't place him. I wonder if he's visited Boston before. I'm sure I've seen him some place."

"Now that you mention it, I think I've seen him somewhere before, too."

"His name doesn't sound familiar, though. I've never met or heard of a Chad Johnson before."

"Neither have I."

"He must look like someone we've seen, maybe an intern who spent time training here."

"That's probably it."

"Why isn't this Cindy here by his side? Something just doesn't add up."

"Maybe they're estranged."

"You'd better forget about him, Tash. He might be from a crime family or something. It's really weird that he'd end up here. He's obviously hiding from some people who might be trying to kill him."

"You're probably right, Jess. It was all in jest, anyway. Come on, let's go to lunch." she tugged at her arm.

*　*　*

Dottie approached one of the tables near the front door where four grey-haired men were congregated. Wiping remnants of tomato soup from their chins, they reached for the day-old doughnuts she placed before them.

"Haven't seen him for a couple of weeks." the man with the grey toque and torn fisherman's pullover said, "Hasn't showed up at the rooming house, either. Landlord wants to throw his stuff out

245

with the trash. I put it all in my room in case, you know, he comes back. There might be some important papers he needs in there.”

“Nobody's seen ‘im on the streets either. I've been askin’.” a thinner man spoke, ramming half a sugar doughnut into his mouth.

“Maybe he should be reported missing.” Dottie suggested, “Your friend might have met with some unfortunate circumstances. He might be at the hospital or something. You should tell the police.”

“Cops don't like us.” a heavy-set man with red cheeks laughed, “They'd lock us up for no reason.”

“Do you want me to report it for you? Then, at least, you might be able to find out what's happened.”

“That's mighty nice of you, Ma'am.” the fourth man tipped his baseball cap.

“Just wait till I get a pen and some paper.” Dottie ran back to the kitchen, grabbed the notepad and pen on the counter used for making lists of required supplies, and returned to the group. She pulled up a chair beside them. “What's your friend's name?”

“Billy.”

“His last name?”

“We just know him as Billy.” one man shrugged, “Don't know his last name.”

“That's okay. Where's the rooming house where he lives?”

“555 Brunswick Street. It's the big old brown house.”

“Who's the landlord?”

“Big Al. Albert Burgess.”

“What are Billy's habits, hangouts?”

“He hangs out outside the used book store on King Street. On nice days, he sits on the bench, reading the newspaper. People around there know him and give him old newspapers. Billy likes to do the puzzles. During inclement weather, he's in "The White Owl Café". The owner, Suzanne, takes good care of him, gives him free food and coffee."

"What does he look like?"

"You seen 'im in here. He's the strappin' young fella."

"Tall, blond, looks in his mid-thirties?"

"That's him. That's our Billy."

"Dottie!" a petite brunette in a Bohemian dress called out from the kitchen, "Your cousin's here to pick you up."

"Thanks, Holly." she rose and reassured the men, "Don't worry. I'll give this information to the police. We'll find out what's happened to your friend."

"Thank you, Ma'am. Have a good day."

"You have a good day, too. See you next weekend." she waved on her way to the kitchen, where Tony was waiting.

She removed her apron and hung it up on its hook beside the other volunteers' aprons. Tearing off the sheets with her writing, she returned the pen and notepad to the counter and placed the sheets in her handbag.

"Today's the day." she said to Tony, "I think it's going to be good for her to get away. Staying around here is a constant reminder of Jack."

"She needs a fresh start."

"Who else is coming to see her off?"

"Brett and Peggy are waiting in the car. Warren took her and her parents to the airport in his car. I think Greeney's bringing Daisy and Maggie."

"I think I have a solid lead, Tony. I'll share it with you guys after the plane takes off. Bye, Holly, see you next weekend!" she called out to the woman restocking the freezer.

"Bye, Dottie. Take care." she smiled.

They walked out to the car. Brett waved at them from the front passenger's seat. Dottie slid into the back seat beside Peggy. The sun was peeking out from behind the clouds. Snowbanks were melting into rivulets. Patches of yellow grass on white lawns were winking mischievously. Tony turned on the radio. Helen Reddy's rich voice filled the car with her tender rendition of "You're My World". Dottie leaned back and closed her eyes. Helen Reddy soothed her into a peaceful slumber in the warmth and safety of the car filled with her loved ones.

Continued in Book Three: SUMMER IS A SHORT SEASON

About The Author:

Summer Seline Coyle has a B.A. in Sociology and English Literature, and a certificate in Counselling.

Her personal history of extreme abuse, neglect, and injustice is the driving force behind the empathy, tenderness, and passion in her portrayal of her diverse characters. Through her fiction, she hopes to raise public awareness, and be a healing voice for other survivors.

Other Books By Summer Seline Coyle:

DAISIES FROM ASHES

SCORPIONS HUNT BY NIGHT

SUMMER IS A SHORT SEASON

SUMMER'S ECHO (formerly SANCTUARY)